OFFICE PRESERVES

GALEN SURLAK-RAMSEY

A Tiny Fox Press Book

Tiny Fox Press and the book fox logo are all registered trademarks of Tiny Fox Press LLC

Tiny Fox Press LLC
North Port, FL

For Steph, who doesn't know what a quail is

CHAPTER ONE

Welcome to Preser Tech," says a pair of blurry, red high heels. "We're glad to have you aboard!"

Toby groans and rubs his eyes. A cold marble floor presses into his face, and a small puddle of drool clings to his mouth and cheek. Thankfully, he sees that the shoes hadn't actually done the talking. There's a female attached to them.

The thought churns in his head. *There's a female attached to them.* Toby winces as he pushes himself up and wipes his mouth. "God, my head hurts."

"Oh, don't worry," the woman replies with a laugh. "You're not the first to get a little bump on the noggin."

Toby furrows his brow as he tries to remember what happened, but he only draws a blank. He looks the woman over, hoping that she'll spark something in his memory. Judging from her accent, she's from Minnesota, and going by her boundless energy, she's downed a twelve pack of Red Bull and chased it with a couple lines of cocaine. Her dark eyes promise desire. Her lips promise fulfillment. Her body curves everywhere it should, and her tummy is flat as a board. A sweet fragrance drifts from her skin and tantalizes Toby's nose. Men, no doubt, fawn over her every day. Smooth ones. Rugged ones. Ones that go on twenty-mile fun runs and bench cars with one arm.

"Where am I?" he asks.

"You're in the lobby!'" she replies, extending a hand.

Toby gives her a handshake and smiles to be polite. Concern mounts that his amnesia might be due to a head injury. He reaches up and discovers a large knot near his left temple.

"Feeling okay?" the woman asks.

"Hoping I don't have a concussion," he says. Toby pats down his pockets, and while he can feel his wallet sitting in his right, both his keys and cell phone are missing from his left. "Son of a bitch."

"What's wrong?" the woman asks.

Toby shakes his head. "Not sure where my keys and phone are," he says. "Or my wife and kids, for that matter."

"Oh, don't worry about silly things like that," she says with a dismissive wave of her hand. "I'm sure they're fine."

"Easy for you to say," he says, looking around. The lobby is sparsely decorated. A few cheap, plastic benches are bolted to the floor, and a handful of generic pictures with no related theme hang from the walls. "You said this is Preser Tech?"

"Yup!"

"Where's that?"

"Here, silly."

Toby shakes his head in frustration. "No. Where is here?"

"First floor," she answers. "The lobby."

Toby sighs. "Do you at least know where I parked?"

The woman stares at him blankly. "What?"

"Where I parked my car," he says. When the woman still doesn't react, he tacks on, "You know, how I got here?"

"Oh. Duh," she says with a laugh. "Freddie brought you in."

Toby is about to ask, "Who?" but stops himself when he gets a good look at her clothes. Her red skirt, two sizes too big, hangs loosely off her hips. Her blouse, though tailored, is marred by old stains and has two small tears in the right shoulder. Mismatched diamond studs sit in her ears, and a glance down shows that even the shoes she wears aren't from the same pair.

Toby steps back, wondering which is worse, that someone would come dressed like this to work, or that her employer wouldn't mind. Either way, sticking around to solve his memory lapse is no longer in Toby's itinerary. "It's been nice talking to you, but I need to go."

"Great idea! Let's get you to work!" she says, bouncing on the balls of her feet.

"No, I mean I need to be somewhere else."

"I totally know what you mean," she says. "You already missed the morning meeting."

"You don't understand. I don't work here."

"Aw, I think someone's still sleepy," she replies. "Why don't you get some coffee?"

"Yeah, nice meeting you."

Toby steps away. Behind him, a pair of tinted, glass double doors give a glimpse of the outside world. He can't see much of the street, let alone where his car is parked, but it has to be out there somewhere. He hurries to the exit. His Rockports echo loudly throughout the lobby. He tries the doors, but they don't budge. Toby snorts and tries them again. This time he's more forceful, more panicked.

The doors hold fast.

Toby turns slowly around. "I think they're locked."

"Those don't open," the woman says, now sitting behind a semicircular desk. "Display only. Dangerous out there, you know."

Toby marches over to demand his release, but before he says a word, the woman slides him a food-laden paper plate.

"Have a cookie," she says.

Toby eyes the snacks warily. "No, thank you."

She turns the plate. "Or a candy."

"I'm not hungry."

The plate turns once again. "Rice Krispies Treat?"

Toby hesitates, and the woman grins. "You want one," she says, nudging it forward. "Go on. They're not poison." She breaks a corner off one of the treats and pops it into her mouth. "See?"

"Melissa, is it?" he says, glancing at her nameplate. "I don't have time to play games. Open the doors."

The woman sticks out her lower lip in a very alluring, pouty way. "I really can't let you out, even if I wanted to. I told you, those doors never open. But if you have a treat, I'll point you in the right direction."

Toby sighs and gives in. If it gets him closer to leaving, he decides he can indulge the request. He snags the nearest treat and takes a bite. It's crunchy. It's sweet. It's absolutely delicious. His mouth waters. His taste buds burst in delight. He shuts his eyes and chews. His body warms, and his muscles relax. Worries vanish and he craves more. More! More! MORE!

Toby reaches for another and another. The receptionist smiles as he stuffs his face. Soon, he's munching on the very last treat.

"Yummy, huh?" she says.

Toby nods, not wanting to interrupt marshmallow goodness with a bunch of talk. A stupid, happy smile spreads across his face and his eyes glaze.

"You'll want to go to the fourth floor."

Toby stares at her. His mind feels foggy, and he's unsure what he wants, but her suggestion sounds good. "And the elevators are...?"

"Behind me."

Toby peers around the divider that separates the lobby from whatever else lies beyond. Sure enough, elevator doors stand nestled between a wall full of soda, cracker, and cookie dispensing devices. The neon colors splashed on their sides threaten to burn out Toby's retinas, but he can't look away. A dazzling array of goodies inside the machines' transparent bellies beckon him closer and make him reach for his wallet.

"There are more machines upstairs," Melissa says. "Some have Rice Krispies Treats too."

"More?"

"Lots more."

Toby nods.

"Well, off you go," she says with a shoo. "You're going to love it here."

The elevator dings, and the doors slide open. Toby, now happily nursing an ice-cold Sprite, is about to enter when someone thumps his shoulder.

"Let's have word, yes?" a voice from behind says in a heavy Russian accent.

Toby turns and sees a guard standing with crossed arms. The man's pants, black and fitted, are ironed and creased. Muscles bulge beneath a short-sleeved, blue shirt, while pepper spray, cuffs, and a chrome-plated magnum revolver hang from his belt. Light glints off his bald head, and his eyebrows look like they are made of steel wool.

"Is there a problem?" Toby asks.

"You might say that," the guard replies. He sticks a foot in front of the elevator doors and keeps them from closing. "I saw you talk to Melissa."

"The receptionist?" Toby says, glancing over his shoulder.

"Yes, Melissa. She is my girl."

"Oh no. It wasn't like that," he says, realizing the misunderstanding. "She was only helping."

"You say I am liar?" The guard steps forward. He's still a couple feet away, but even at that distance, his rank breath is nearly overpowering. "Next time you try and steal Boris's girl, I break your neck."

Toby's Krispy-induced bliss washes away under a deluge of adrenaline. He wonders how little it might take to spark a fight with the man—a fight he is certain he will lose, and lose badly.

"Got it, she's Boris's girl," he says, sidestepping into the elevator. "I think I'll be going now.

"Yes, I think you will." Boris removes his foot, and the elevator doors slide shut.

Toby quickly pushes the button to the fourth floor and exhales sharply.

Toby cautiously exits the elevator and steps into a long hall that stretches in either direction. Florescent lighting hums overhead, and the faint scent of cleaner hangs in the air. The walls are painted a light blue, and there are countless spots were previous damage has been haphazardly patched.

Unsure which direction to go, Toby heads right. He passes a pair of bathrooms and an empty break room before stopping at a set of double doors to his left. From behind them, he can hear muffled voices and hopes whoever is in there can help.

Toby cracks the door open and peers inside. A coffee machine bubbles on a nearby folding table and gives a pleasant aroma. Little Richard's "Long Tall Sally" plays from an unseen radio, and the majority of the workspace is filled with cubicles. In, on, and around these cubicles are paper notices of every kind. Some are tacked to the walls. Others hang from bulletin boards. A few are even taped to chairs. Most he can't read due to the distance involved, but the ones he can make out deal with various policy changes.

"Door!" someone shouts.

Instantly, two dozen people pop their heads over the dividers. They each look about with wide eyes and quick jerks of the head. When they spot Toby, they smile and sink back into their cubbies.

"Can someone help me?" Toby says, cautiously stepping inside. "I'm trying to get out of the building, and—"

"Toby?" someone says. "Dude! Is that you?"

Toby snaps his head to the left, astounded anyone knows his name.

A man in his mid-twenties, wearing khaki shorts and a black polo shirt, strides down one of the dividing aisles. "Hell yeah!" he says with a fist pump. "It is you!"

Toby hesitates, trying to place who this person is. "Matt?" he says. "Matt from IT?"

"Dude!" Matt says with shock. "You forgot me already?"

Toby shakes his head. "Sorry, but you were only with us for a week before you went AWOL."

"Naw. Not AWOL. Crashed in bed one night and woke up here."

"But that was a month ago," Toby says. His mind reels at the implications. His stomach knots, and he has a sudden, inexplicable craving for a Rice Krispies Treat.

"No, not a month," Matt says as he scratches his head. "Two, I think. It's hard to keep track. You know, sucky calendars here and all."

"No, I don't know," Toby says. He looks around, worried about who is listening. No one is, but Toby lowers his voice anyway. "You've been stuck here for two months?"

Matt laughs. Loudly. "Stuck?" he says. "As if! This place is sick!"

Toby's hand reaches back for the door. Part of him is convinced this is a dream, and he ought to sit back and enjoy the ride. The other part, however, is screaming at the very real nature of it all and is demanding his exit, post haste.

"Dude, calm down," Matt says. "I totally get what you're going through. Freaked me out at first too."

"This place is not normal."

"Dude, I know," he says, grinning. "The second I got here and met freak girl and her moose, I was sure I was getting axed. Must have spent a good hour or two trying to bail, but then I realized what they got and stayed."

"I don't care what they have," says Toby. "I want out."

"Dude, they've got free rooms to sleep, movies to watch and—"

"I don't care."

"A gym. A mall—"

"I don't care!" Toby takes a deep breath and fights the urge to lash out. It's a tough fight, but he knows going down that path usually complicates matters in the same way a tornado touching down on the family car complicates a picnic. So Toby tries his best to stay in control and reason with his acquaintance. "Don't you want to go home? See your friends? Your family? Hell, go surf?"

"And give up this epic place?" Matt scoffs. "No way. Dude, I got two secretaries, free room and grub, and—"

"Wait," Toby interrupts. "You've got _two_ secretaries?"

Matt grins and looks over his shoulder. "Yeah, and Clarice is practically a doe."

Toby follows Matt's gaze until it intersects with two small desks that are sitting in front of a private office. One of the desks is unoccupied, but behind the other sits a redhead, fit and freckled, who is reading a magazine. "Why do you have two secretaries?" Toby says, realizing he's staring at her a little too long. "You're an entry-level tech."

"I'm Assistant Chief Tech of Marketing and Development of Strategic Positions in Volatile Environments," Matt proudly replies. He throws a thumb toward his office door. "Check out the nameplate, brah."

Toby squints. "What does that even mean?"

"Hell if I know. Some kook had it before me."

"And?"

"And what? He got transferred or something. I ripped his office before some wanna-be could. Once I had that, bagging a couple secretaries was cake. It's all about the tag. Longer the better, and that's pretty damn long."

"No, I mean, what do you do here?"

Matt beams like he came off a kamikaze wave. "I go deep, graze, and enjoy life."

"And you need secretaries to do that because...?"

"Brah, don't hate," Matt says, crossing his arms over his chest. "Not cool."

"I'm not hating," Toby replies. "I'm not. This place is creepy."

"I hear you, brah." Matt leans in close. "But let me clue you in. Get yourself a sec before people think you're a poser. All the bunnies are taken, but they're not all swamp donkeys."

"Keep the secretaries. How do I get home?"

"Freddie's the only one who can make that happen," Matt replies.

Toby cocks his head at the first mention of anyone specific that could help him out. "Who?"

"Oh, dude!" Matt says with a bright smile. "You don't know Freddie? He's boss!"

"He is the boss or he is boss?" Toby asks.

"Both!" Matt then chuckles. "But don't flail when you see him."

"I'm not going to do anything other than demand my immediate release," says Toby. "And he better let me out or so help me God I'll punch him in the face."

Matt looks over Toby's shoulder and his eyes light up. "Freddie!"

CHAPTER TWO

Toby turns and finds himself face-to-face with a thing that looks like a hideous mix of snake, man, and spider. The creature supports itself on a serpentine tail, while a second tail, complete with a four-fingered hand at its end, floats lazily behind. Leathery, grey skin covers its torso and reflects the light, making it look slick. A pair of slender arms hangs from its side, but they have enough muscle definition to hint at some strength. Atop its body sits an elongated head covered in short, spiked hairs. Eight beady, black eyes stare deeply into Toby's soul, and a pair of fangs covers the creature's mouth.

Words fail to pass from Toby's terror-stricken lips. He jumps back and crashes into a divider wall before hitting the ground.

"Dude, stop acting like that," Matt says, one hand partially covering his face. "You're embarrassing me."

Toby wants to run. His mind demands it, but his body refuses. With effort, he manages a single question. "What the holy hell is that?"

A high-pitched burbling comes out of Freddie's mouth. It's quickly replaced by an intelligible voice, but sounds as if it has been digitally processed and harmonized several times over. "Hi there," he says, extending a hand. Clutched inside that hand is a Rice Krispies Treat. "See it? Huh? Huh? You can have it, if you want."

Toby doesn't reply, and Freddie pats Toby on the head. "It's okay, little persie. I bet your friend would like one."

A flick of Freddie's wrist sends the treat arcing through the air. Matt promptly snatches it and devours the snack in less than a second. A moment later, Matt is smiling, drooling, and bouncing on the balls of his feet.

Freddie leans close to Toby's face and locks his eight eyes with Toby's two. "Do you understand me?"

Toby's brain begins to reengage, but barely. "P-Persie?"

"Persie. Person. We're friendly here at your new home, Toby. We are family after all."

Freddie's words ring in Toby's ears. The thought of his wife and children spurs him into action. He shoots up and pushes away from both Freddie and Matt. His eyes dart around, searching for the exit. "Get away from me."

Matt's face sours. "Dude, knock it off."

"Shut up. I'm getting the hell out of here."

"You don't want to go," Freddie says. "We'd miss you so."

"I said shut up," Toby yells. His eyes catch sight of a nearby pen, and he scoops it up. Small, red, and plastic, it's not even remotely as dangerous as a knife or a gun, but as far as Toby is concerned, he can slay a dragon with it. "Let me out. Now."

Freddie shakes his head, and though Toby isn't sure, he thinks he can see a hint of sadness in the arachnid face. "Aw, you must be hurt and scared," Freddie says. "I understand. I can make it all better."

Toby jabs the pen in the air a few times and inches toward the doors. "Come near me and I'll punch this right through your fat, hairy head."

"You're not being a good Toby, Toby," Freddie says. His voice is soft, but holds an edge of command. "Now sit."

Toby ignores him and continues to move. "I don't know what kind of sick joke this is, but I'm ending it now."

Freddie looks behind Toby and makes a gesture with his hand. In a flash, Toby is hit from behind, and he finds himself pressed into blue-purple carpet. Shouting fills the office air, both his and others. Hands wrestle his own behind his back and bind them together.

"Get the hell off me!" Toby screams, still trying to break free.

Something pushes into his back with the weight of a dozen elephants and knocks the air out of him.

"Calm down, persie. This is for your own good," Freddie says. "This will only hurt for a second."

Toby gasps for air and manages to spit out a gratifying, "Fuck you."

Freddie makes a garbled call from his mouth and the pressure on Toby's back is lifted. Before he can get up, he feels a pair of pricks in his side. A heartbeat later, his body goes rigid, and his muscles spasm. Forty-two convulsions later, it stops.

A boot prods his ribs.

Toby lies still, his mind unable to register anything else.

When Toby's brain awakens, he realizes he's seated in a high-back, leather chair inside an office. A wall clock says it's four in the afternoon. Plastic ties cut into his wrists and bind them to the armrests. Given the pain racing up his legs, he suspects his ankles have been bound as well. In front of him is an oak desk, void of anything save a desk lamp and a Fisher-Price telephone. On the other side is Freddie, who has his hands behind his back and is stroking his chin with the digits on his tail.

"Do you like your office?" Freddie asks. "Look how big and shiny it is."

Toby ignores both the spaciousness of the room and the sheen on the walls. Instead, he pulls against the restraints with all his strength and succeeds in having them dig more into his skin. Finally, Toby stops his struggle and looks Freddie square in the eyes. "Let me go, you freak."

Matt appears at Freddie's side and shrugs apologetically. "My bad, man. I told him not to flail."

Freddie turns and pats Matt's head. "You concerned about your buddy? Don't worry. He's in good hands."

"I want to go home!" Toby shouts. When that doesn't get a reaction out of either Freddie or Matt, Toby thrashes around. The restraints still hold, still cut into his skin, and after a great deal of exertion, all Toby's managed to do is drench himself in sweat.

Freddie sits down on the edge of the desk and sighs. "Settle down, Toby, or you won't get a secretary."

A growl slips from Toby's mouth.

"Look at all the fun persie stuff we have for you," Freddie says, leaning back. "We've got apartments to sleep in, movies to watch, a gym to use, and a mall with all the stores you love."

"I've heard all this before," Toby says, eyes narrowing into his best death-to-you look he can muster.

"Of course you have," he says. "But I bet you didn't know we have all the paperwork you want, did you?"

Toby, caught off guard by the bizarre comment, momentarily loses his hostility. "Paperwork?"

"Oh yes, Toby," says Freddie. "We've got more forms than you can dream of that need to be signed, stamped, and filed. Doesn't that sound wonderful?"

Toby shakes his head. His muscles twitch, but he doesn't pull against the restraints. Brute force, he's beginning to realize, is going to get him nowhere. He'll have to figure another way out. "Going home sounds wonderful. You can't keep me here."

"Of course I can," Freddie replies without missing a beat. "Beings from across the galaxy pay good money to come find you in your natural habitat. That's something even you can understand."

Toby's stomach flips several times over. His body numbs, and the only thing he can feel is his heart hammering inside his chest. His eyes glaze and his voice is but a whisper. "I can't spend the rest of my life in a zoo."

"Don't be such a pouty little Toby," Freddie says, merrily. "We're not a zoo. We're a preserve! The best one in the galaxy!"

"My wife..." Toby says, still drowning in thoughts. "My kids..."

"Oh, they'll be fine," Freddie says, getting up and snaking his way in front of the desk. "Your wife is probably mating with another office manager this moment. And guess what, Toby? I'm going to make you the VP of Communications and Investment Opportunities for the Acquisition of Hostile Companies. You wouldn't want a boring family to mess that up, would you? Look how long this nametag is."

Toby snaps back to the here and now at the alien's offer. His body dumps adrenaline into his system like a B-52 dumps munitions on goat herders.

Toby surges forward. The ties cut deeper into his arms, drawing blood. At first, Freddie is expressionless, but when the chair cracks and Toby jolts forward, Freddie straightens and rises high on his tail. Towering over Toby, he grabs him by the shirt collar and pushes him down. "Listen to me, Toby," he says. "If you don't settle down, I can't let you work with the others."

"I don't want to work with the others."

Freddie leans in. "Employees that can't get along get terminated."

The alien's warning is not lost on Toby, and he forces himself to relax. "Fine," he says through gritted teeth.

"You're not going to be a bad Toby once I let you free, are you?"

"Do I at least get a secretary today?" Toby asks, hoping his budding deception will play to his advantage.

Freddie nods. "I bet Matt will give you one of his, won't you Matt?"

Matt jumps up from a seat he had taken. "Whoa! Dude!"

"Down, persie," Freddie says without even a glance to the protesting surfer. "I'll get you a new one. Maybe even two."

Matt raises an eyebrow, clearly intrigued by the offer. "Two?"

Freddie strokes the back of Matt's head and scratches him behind the ears. "Soon as the next batch gets here, you bet."

"That is pure sex," Matt says, beaming. He throws a nod toward the door and continues. "Take Clarice."

Freddie produces a Rice Krispies Treat and places it on the table. "See Toby?" he says, nudging it forward. "I'm here to help."

The ties around Toby's wrists loosen, and he pulls free. He has no idea how it happened, for both Freddie and Matt are still a good pace or two away, but he's grateful nonetheless.

Freddie nudges the treat. "Go on, boy. Take it."

Toby warily takes the treat and pops it into his mouth. Saliva pours into his mouth, and a bit even escapes the corners of his mouth as he chews. To his right, a dozen people are pressed against the outside of the office's full-length window, staring at Toby with curiosity.

Toby's mind finds a warm, happy place and settles in, thinking about blankets fresh from the dryer and sips of hot cocoa. His gaze drifts from the window to Freddie.

Freddie. Good ole Freddie. Such a nice, caring fellow, even if his looks would have caused Medusa to faint. But looks aren't everything, Toby reminds himself. Beauty is in the eye of the beholder, and Mrs. Freddie, whoever she was, was probably fond of him.

"One more treat before supper?" asks Freddie.

Toby licks his lips at the thought of dinner. Certainly meals here must be marvelous if the treats are so delicious. He doesn't want to spoil his appetite, but decides one more snack wouldn't hurt. "Yeah," he says. "That would be great."

Freddie turns to Matt. "Fetch Clarice so she can meet her new boss," he says. "Have her pick up a treat along the way."

Matt nods and bounds out the office like a puppy.

"I have to go now, Toby," Freddie says, patting Toby's head. "Clarice will have you completely ready for the start of a new season."

Season? The thought churns in Toby's mind as Freddie leaves the room. He's not sure what season it is, or if it's important, or if he should even care. To the latter, Toby decides he doesn't. Whether Freddie meant football or basketball, fall or winter, Toby lets the topic drop from his mind. All he really wants is another treat.

Toby's office door opens and in steps a young woman. She sports two-inch heels that bring her to a whopping five-six in height, a tan skirt that is mostly stain-free, and red hair put in a smartly made bun. Her face, light skinned with a few freckles, is blank.

At first, Toby wonders how long it's been since she smiled. When she turns to face him directly, however, all thoughts vanish. He's stuck staring at a jagged scar that runs from the top of her forehead, through a dead right eye, and to the bottom of her right jaw.

The woman places a snack on his desk and says, "Your Rice Krispies Treat, Mister...?" Her voice trails. Toby doesn't answer since he's still gawking at her scar. A puzzled look crosses her face. "Would you like to stare at it more, Mister...?"

"No," he says, face reddening from embarrassment. "Sorry. Call me Toby."

"Okay, Mr. Toby."

"No, just Toby," he says. "Mister is my father."

The woman perks in posture and tone. "Father? You have a father?"

"Of course I do. Doesn't everyone?"

The woman laughs. "Of course you do," she says. Her words come faster now. "Everyone has a father. Everyone. You too. We all do. But you know who he is, don't you?"

"Why wouldn't I?" he replies. His brow furrows. Anger builds. Krispy-induced euphoria starts fading away. "In fact, I've got a wife and kids too."

The woman grabs his hand and shakes it vigorously. "Clarice," she says. "My name is Clarice. He said you'd come, said if I waited long enough you'd show. You've no idea how long I've waited for you, Toby."

"Who are you?" Toby asks, instinctively grabbing the treat off the desk.

"No!" Clarice shouts.

But it's too late. Toby has the treat crammed in his mouth and is chewing slowly. Happiness washes over him, and he manages to get out a garbled, "What?"

"Oh no, no, no," she says. "This is bad. You can't leave me, too."

Toby finishes his snack. "Is something the matter?"

Clarice grabs him by the shoulders and looks square in his eyes. "Your wife. Tell me about her. Quick."

"Oh, she's nice," Toby says. He looks down, sad at his empty hands. "Do you have another treat on you?"

Clarice mutters under her breath. Toby isn't sure what it was she said, but he hopes it doesn't have anything to do with a Rice Krispies shortage.

"So, about that treat..." says Toby.

"Treat, yes," she says, letting go of his shoulders and backing up. "I can get you a treat. I will. Just...just don't go anywhere. I'll be right back."

"Please do so." Toby eases into his chair and kicks his feet up on his desk. "You are my secretary, after all. I can't be doing all this paperwork on an empty stomach."

"Coffee too? We've got good coffee. Great coffee." she says. She nervously bites the knuckle on her fist and taps her foot.

"No, I don't think so."

"You want coffee," she says. "You have to have it. Have to."

Clarice exits the room, and Toby looks outside his office window as he awaits her return. The crowd that was watching Toby has now moved several feet away while Freddie stands nearby with another alien by his side. This creature looks similar to Freddie, though it's taller and has tentacles dangling from its shoulders. Freddie and Mr. Squid (for that is what Toby names him) meander through the crowd, talking amongst themselves and occasionally poking the office workers with a finger.

"I brought six," Clarice says, drawing Toby's attention. She slides a plate full of yummy goodness onto the desk with one hand while holding a large Styrofoam cup with the other.

"Thanks." Toby takes the nearest treat and shoves it into his mouth. "What are they doing out there?"

"Inspection," she answers. "Inspection for the season. They always do that the day before. Always."

"Will they come in here?"

"Everyone gets inspected. Everyone has to be perfect."

A dozen heartbeats later, Freddie slithers in with Mr. Squid in tow. Clarice stiffens, and her face loses all emotion. Toby snacks on another treat and decides all of the world's problems could be solved with the right amount of sugar.

"Up, Toby," says Freddie.

Toby instantly obeys.

Freddie and Mr. Squid talk back and forth in a high-pitched, barely audible language that feels like a cat is scratching the inside of Toby's ears. Eventually, Mr. Squid extends a tentacle. It slips around Toby's ribs and up his back. Toby giggles as it slides through his hair.

"Good, Toby," says Freddie. "Good, good boy."

Mr. Squid uses his other tentacle to gently push Toby's head back and open his mouth. For the next several seconds, Mr. Squid looks inside before sticking an appendage in and tapping a few of Toby's teeth. Though awkward, the ordeal ends and Mr. Squid and Freddie exit the room, chattering away in their alien language.

"Here's your coffee," Clarice says, setting it on the table.

Toby smiles. "That went well, don't you think?"

Clarice glances over her shoulder. She then turns back around, the nerves in her body and voice instantly resurfacing. "Drink the coffee. Quick. You've got to be quick."

Toby picks up the cup and opens the lid. Inside is the darkest liquid he's ever seen. "Black?"

"Very. Very black."

"Could you add some sugar and crème?" he asks. "Maybe dissolve a treat or two in it as well?"

Clarice shakes her head. "No. No. It has to be black. He made me promise it would always be black."

Toby balks.

"Please drink it. There's not much time left."

Toby takes a sip, remembering that the last time someone had him try something—namely Melissa downstairs—it turned out well. The liquid is smooth and coats everything it touches. The taste is bitter. Unique. Toby takes another sip, a larger one. Finally, still curious about it all, he downs the whole thing in a few gulps. His belly questions his judgment.

"Oh, Toby," Freddie says, making an unexpected return. "I have something for you."

Toby leans forward, not because he's interested in what Freddie has to say, but because a cramp is now building in his abdomen.

"Toby?" Freddie says.

Clarice steps to the side and not a moment too soon.

Toby opens his mouth and empties the contents of his stomach. Neither desk, nor floor, nor Freddie is spared.

"Oh, god," Toby says, horrified.

"Toby!" Freddie barks.

Clarice quickly positions herself between the two. "I'll take care of him, Freddie," she says. "I'll make him clean. Clean is good. Sexy."

Freddie backs up and looks himself over. "Good girl, Clarice," he says. "Be fast about it, will you? The nursery's been slow, lately."

"I will," Clarice replies.

Freddie leaves, flinging bits of puke off his body as he goes.

Toby wipes his mouth and winces as a headache forms. "Oh, god, I feel like crap."

"Come on," Clarice says, pulling him by his belt loop and leading him out. "We're getting the hell out of here."

CHAPTER THREE

Clarice pulls Toby down the hall and shoves him into the elevator. Its doors close, and it begins to rise. The sudden shift of the floor causes Toby to stumble. He catches himself on his knees, and his stomach empties once more.

"Dear Jesus," he says, staring at his hands. Bits of goop cling to each one, but it's not the vomit that's bothering him as much the fact that portions of his hands are stained an inky black. "I think I'm dying."

The doors open, and Clarice yanks him out of the elevator and into a long hall painted a light yellow that smells like cleaner. "You're not dying," she says, dragging him along. "Not dying at all."

Toby's stomach knots and sends a stab of pain through his nervous system, convincing him otherwise. "You're not the one coughing up black crap."

"You're not dying. I wouldn't do that to you," she says. They come to a stop in front of an off-white door. She whips out a plastic keycard from her pocket and slides it through an electronic lock. The door chirps, and Toby hears the lock disengage. "Get inside. It'll all be better soon."

Clarice opens the door for him, and he steps into a small apartment. Or rather, Toby believes there's a small apartment hidden under the total mess he is now taking in. From beneath countless baby and parenting magazines, he thinks he can make out a sofa nearby. Short, grey carpet covers the floor and is currently being kept warm by a surplus of mismatched clothes and a handful of Cabbage Patch dolls. To his side is a waste paper basket filled with the hollow shells of broken Bic pens, and at the other end of the room, a battered air conditioner hums loudly.

Clarice opens a side door and thrusts Toby into a bathroom that makes the lavatory on a DC-9 look like the Taj Mahal. How the two are actually fitting inside, Toby decides, defies the laws of physics. "Rinse," she says, handing him a small plastic cup. "Flush the toner."

Toby complies, and once he's done using both sink and cup, he looks up at her and says, "Toner?"

"I put toner in your coffee," she explains as if it was nothing more than a cube or two of sugar. "But don't worry. Don't worry. The worst has passed. An hour, maybe two...maybe two. You'll be okay. It's always okay."

Toby grits his teeth as he fights another wave of nausea. "You spiked my coffee?"

Clarice shakes her head and bites her knuckle. "I had to," she says, shaking. "Had to. There wasn't a choice. It was that or ink. Ink works also, but not as well."

Toby coughs. Spits. Black-tinged saliva sticks to the counter and the mirror on the wall. He takes a look at himself, at his teeth, specifically, and is revolted by their dingy color. He grips the counter and wants to strangle the woman where she stands. "What kind of sick freak are you?"

Clarice grabs his hands. Her words spit out like bullets from a machine gun. "Don't be mad, Toby. I'm helping. That's all I'm doing, trying to help. Trying to save us."

"You had me drink toner," he says, body temperature rising.

"No, no. You don't understand. You have to understand." She straightens. Her eyes brighten and she smiles. "It's the drugs, Toby. That's what this is for. Adrenaline helps, but not for long. That's why toner is best." She hugs herself tightly and rocks. "See? I'm helping you so we can escape."

"What drugs?"

"The treats, the food," she says. "They're all drugged. They tried with the water, but it makes it taste funny. People wouldn't drink it."

Toby shakes his head. "No way. I'd know."

"No, no," she says. "No one notices. Most are lost after a few snacks. Two days, tops, and they're gone. Always gone." She smiles broadly and gives him a big squeeze. "But not you! You're not one of them. Not yet. And that's good. Good for us both. You have to see that. You have to believe me."

Toby fills the cup twice more and rinses his mouth out each time. His stomach joins the fun and pukes again, prompting him to rinse and repeat for a third and final time. "You're out of your mind."

"It's a preserve," she says, eyes narrowed. "A preserve! They're the enemy. Not me...not me."

Her words stew in Toby's brain. It doesn't take long for him to admit that she's the most normal person he's met here, and even if she did poison his coffee, she's also talking about an escape, which Toby finds instantly appealing. "Fine. I'm sorry. Tell me you have a plan to get out of this nightmare."

Clarice smiles. "I do. We planned for a long time. Long time."

"Fill me in," he says.

"Not now. Too many questions, not enough time," she replies, taking his hands in hers. Her voice softens along with her face. "Play your role. Do as I say."

Toby concedes that his mountain of questions might grow tenfold if she answers any of them. Besides, all he really wants is to get home in one piece. "If it means escaping, I'm all yours."

Clarice smiles broadly and lets go. "You have no idea how relieved I am hearing that. No idea."

"What do you need from me?"

"First, take a shower," she says. "You reek."

Toby laughs. "Where? Here?"

Clarice nods and points to a small shower massage that's hanging on the wall behind him. "Use that," she says. "The floor is tiled. The drain is under the sink. Soap is in the medicine cabinet."

Toby looks under the counter and sure enough, there's a tiny drain. "I can't believe this doubles as a shower. What do I do about clothes?"

"Toss yours," she replies, opening the door and stepping out. "I'll find you better ones, ones that won't make you stand out."

Toby nods and begins to shut the door, but Clarice catches it. "Something else," she says. "Something you can't forget. You mustn't ever forget."

"What?"

"Don't talk about leaving," she says. "What happens here, stays here."

Toby cocks his head to the side. "Like Vegas?"

"They're always watching, always listening," she says. Her eyes dart around and her voice lowers. "Not only Freddie, but the office people, too."

"Surely they want to go home," says Toby.

Clarice shakes her head. "This is home. They're stock. Born and raised here. Except a few they bring to replace those gone. We're the ones the drugs are meant for."

"We can't leave them behind," says Toby. "We've got to save them."

Clarice takes his hands and grips them tight. "No, Toby. You don't understand. They don't want to go. They don't want to leave this life. They'll do anything to keep you from leaving too."

Her tone sends a shiver up his spine, but with a little luck, he figures he won't be around long enough to see whatever she's alluding to. "Okay," Toby says. "No escape talk."

"We'll be okay, Toby," she says. "Don't worry. Shower. Get clean. Then we leave."

Ten minutes later, Toby, dripping wet, peeks out of the door. He's about to ask for a towel when he realizes the apartment has changed. The clothes on the floor have been stuffed in and around a couple of hampers. The magazines are gone, and the lighting has changed from the electric variety to the candle sort. The most notable change, however, is that the sofa is now a bed, a bed in which Clarice is lying on her side, covers drawn.

"Clarice?" Toby asks, unsure what to make of the scene.

"Yes, Toby?"

"Can I get a towel?"

"Sure."

A few moments pass and the only thing Toby gets is a whiff of light perfume. Hairs raise on the back of his neck, and he wonders what happened to the jumpy secretary he'd met a short while ago. "So," he says, uncomfortable in the silence, "about that towel."

"Yes?"

Despite the dim light, he's pretty sure he catches a glimpse of a seductive grin. Or maybe it's more of the hungry type, and given this place so far, the thought crosses his mind that maybe she's the resident black widow. Toby dismisses the thought as paranoia and says, "Can I get one or not?"

Her slender arm escapes the covers. "Toby, you can get a towel any time you like," she says, pointing to a nearby corner. "They're folded right there."

"Look," says Toby. "I'm not entirely comfortable strolling out there naked. Can you grab it for me?"

"I can," Clarice replies. She gracefully slips out of the bed, and that's when Toby realizes the only thing the shadows have to cling to on her is her bare skin.

"Clarice?" he stammers as her toned silhouette approaches. He wants to say something else, something about being married or that being in a zoo doesn't really do it for him, but he gets a second whiff of perfume, and his mind goes bank.

Clarice pulls the door fully open and presses a towel into his chest. "There you go."

"Thanks." He stares, admiring how the bathroom light strikes her every curve.

Clarice snakes her arms around his neck and soon it's not the towel pressing into his chest, but her body. "Since I carried you a towel from the bed," she says, kissing his neck, "you should carry me back."

Toby inhales. A fragrance, sweet and intoxicating, drifts from her neck. His world collapses into the moment. All he can think about, all he can do, is touch her, kiss her.

"Carry me back," she says again.

Toby nods. Her legs wrap around his waist and he brings her to the bed. He rounds the one and only corner between bed and bath a little too quickly, too haphazardly, and stumbles.

Pain stabs through his right foot, and his two smallest toes scream in agony.

"Christ!" Toby yells. He falls forward but manages to keep upright long enough to dump Clarice on the bed and not the floor. He drops to a knee and grabs his foot. Since the light is dim, it's hard to inspect the damage. There are no obvious signs of bruising, but judging by the fire burning in his toes, he prays they aren't fractured.

"Oh, you poor thing," says Clarice. She slides her arms around his chest from behind and nibbles his ear like his bride, Nikki, used to do.

Toby straightens and pushes her away. "Stop," he says, shaking his head while trying to make sense of what's going on.

"Why?" she replies. Confusion mars both her face and voice. She tries to pull him in again and is rebuffed a second time. "What's wrong?"

Toby takes to his feet. His heart thumps loudly in his ears. "I'm married, that's what." He stops as another whiff of perfume enters his nose. His muscles relax. The engine to his libido revs, but his brain, which is saturated with adrenaline and endorphins, plays its trump card and overrides the desire to make her claw the ceiling in ecstasy. "It's your perfume, isn't it?" he says, backing up. "You're trying to drug me like the others."

Clarice takes a bold step forward and doesn't break eye contact under the accusation. "I thought it would help put you in the mood," she says. "I can wash it off, if you like. Then we can start over."

"I'm not starting anything," he says, grabbing a towel from the floor and wrapping it around his waist. "I thought you were trying to help."

Clarice gently takes his wrists. "I am helping. Besides, you know you want to."

"I'm not going to tell you again, I'm married."

"So?" she says without missing a beat. "I'm your secretary now. It's okay."

Toby swipes her hands away. "I said no, and I mean it."

"You don't find me attractive?"

Toby shakes his head, despite the fact that his lower half is screaming, "Yes!"

"Look, it's not like that-" he begins to say, but Clarice catches a sob in her throat and he stops. She might be a touch overly aggressive, but he can't help but feel sorry for her.

"You think I'm ugly," she mumbles. She runs her fingers through her hair and grips the back of her head. "No, no, no," she repeats over and over. She paces and starts to hyperventilate. "You can't. You mustn't."

The panic building in her voice is all that's needed to drop Toby's guard completely. "What?" he asks with genuine concern.

Clarice looks up, hopeful, scared. "You have to sleep with me," she says, eyes watering. "You have to screw me."

Toby retreats the last bit he can before his back presses against the wall. "Look, I don't know what the hell this is all about," he says, hands up, "but you've just joined the ranks of bat-shit crazy, which isn't my kind of girl."

Clarice steps forward again. She paws at his hands, then takes and rubs one against her tear-stained cheek. "No, you don't understand," she says. "They have to smell you on me. They have to know I'm yours."

Toby pushes her away. "I'm leaving."

"You can't," she says, following his retreat with arms out. "You mustn't."

"Watch me."

Clarice freezes. Her mouth hangs open, and whatever it is she's staring at, Toby's certain it's not him. "No, no, no," she whispers, digging her fingernails into her chest. "I can't sit and watch. Not again. Not again."

"Look, when you've calmed down, we can talk," he says.

"Toby!" She says it with such a force that he jumps straight up. "They want you. All of them. You, your title, your job. Everything."

"What are you babbling about?"

"They're going to bag you if you don't listen. You have to listen. You have to stay."

"They do?" he asks, flattered and confused. "Why?"

"You're a buck. Bucks get bagged. It's the way it is."

"I don't care," he says. "I'll turn them down too. All I want is to go home."

Toby goes to walk away, but Clarice grabs his wrists. "Please stay," she says. "Stay for the night. I'll explain it all if you give me a chance."

"No—"

Clarice grabs her head and hunched over, walks in tight circles. "Stupid, stupid, stupid, Clarice," she says. "You've got to be smart. Be smart for me. For us." She stops her pacing and squares off with Toby once more. Her shoulders roll back, her chest up. Her posture is near perfect at this point. "I'm sorry, Toby," she says, voice flat. "I came on too strong, and I apologize. I wasn't lying before, but I need you to stay here and not go outside if we're going to get out of here alive."

Toby shakes his head. This marks the third shift in her behavior he's witnessed since being in her room, and to say that that makes him uneasy is like saying sitting on a burning hot fire poker might make him a little uncomfortable. He can't even begin to fathom someone going from skittish, to horny, to desperate, and back to normal in such a short time.

"This is really creeping me out," he says. He has the urge to bolt but realizes that even if she's a little psycho, if she knows a way out, he should stick around. "Tell me what you've got in mind."

"The aliens have these things," Clarice says, stammering, searching for words. "They use them to open doors. Doors to other places we can't get to. We just need to get a hold of one."

Toby smirks. "You mean they have keys?"

Clarice tosses him a pile of mismatched clothes from the floor and grabs some for herself as well. "I know what keys are," she says, dressing. "And they aren't like car keys. They look like a deck of cards or a cigarette pack. I don't know how they work, but they open these doors, or portals, or whatever you want to call them."

"A portal?"

Clarice nods. "They're flat and appear out of nowhere. Sounds like a portal. Looks like a portal. What do you want to call them?"

Toby concedes the point as he slips on some boxers. "Where do they lead?"

"Out. That's all I know."

"And how do you plan on getting one of these devices?" he asks.

"We take one," she says, putting on a white baby doll shirt. Her voice wavers. "We take one when they watch us mate. The wardens always like to watch."

"This is ridiculous," Toby says. "You think I'm really going to fall for that?"

"No, no, I know," Clarice says, clearly trying to placate him with both body and word. "No sex. You said that, I know. We can get a key though, the two of us, if we work together, give them a show."

Toby raises an eyebrow in skepticism, and he can't help but think she's leading him on another ruse. "How can I possibly trust you?"

Clarice throws her hands up. "I don't know," she says. "I'd do anything I could to make you believe. Anything."

Toby pauses, searching for something the woman could do as a show of trust. "Tell me about your scar."

Clarice backs. Her entire affect goes flat. "What about it?"

"How did you get it?"

"Someone cut me."

"Who?"

"Nick," she says. "My boyfriend." The most uncomfortable of silences settles between the two. "He's not here anymore," she eventually tacks on.

Toby's gut knots, and though the mask she has on her face is nearly impenetrable, he can still catch a glimpse of unspeakable pain in her eyes. "I'm sorry."

Clarice clears her eyes with her hands and nods. "It's not your fault," she says. "And I'm the one that should be apologizing," she adds. "I'm really not a whore."

Toby laughs nervously. "It's not that I didn't enjoy it, but-"

"I know. You're married, and this place is scary," she finishes. She flips a nearby light switch and the room brightens. "Scares me too. Always has."

Now that he can see better, Toby looks down at the oversized t-shirt he's about to put on. It's a grey Nike, and in the center, Toby counts nine small holes clustered together in about a six-inch radius. "This shirt's a little worn," he says, holding it up for her to see. "Got anything without pencil holes driven through it?"

Clarice shakes her head. "New clothes don't come often," she says. "Everything's used. Everything's worn."

"Yeah, but it looks like this thing sat under a leaky engine block," Toby adds, noting the large, discolored section of fibers in the front of the shirt. "Not sure I want to wear rags."

"Put it on," Clarice says. "Only those on top get to wear nice things. Nice things make you stand out. You don't want that."

"Why? Is this like a prison where people beat each other up for clothes?" asks Toby.

"Not a prison," she says. "Worse. It's a preserve. Prisoners are let go. We never are."

Toby looks at her, hoping for a deeper explanation. Not that being kept in an alien zoo for the rest of his life isn't bad enough, but he's not understanding the connection she's trying to make. "What don't I know?"

"Best you stay in the dark," she says with a shudder. "Ignorance is bliss. I've told you all that you need to know." She glances behind him to where a small clock hangs on the wall. "We need to go. Lunch is soon. Get dressed or they'll come looking."

Toby complies, throwing on the holey shirt and putting on a pair of torn blue jeans. He looks himself over and says, "I feel like I'm the fifth in line for hand-me-downs."

Clarice smiles. "That's my plan." She takes his hands in hers and stands in front of him. "Listen close. There are rules for eating. Rules you must obey."

"Rules?"

"Yes, rules," she says. "We made them a long time ago. We have to follow them. You have to follow them. The season starts in the morning, and they'll be there watching us eat, picking us out, making sure we're harmless. So, do what I say. No more, no less."

"Okay, but this would be so much better if you'd tell me what's going on."

Clarice's eyes widen. Her body shivers. "No, no, no," she says, looking down at the ground and shaking her head over and over. "You don't want to know. Pressure will be too much, and we're so close to leaving. When we're home, when we're safe, I'll tell you if you still want to know. But we have to leave before the season starts. And we can't do that if you don't pay attention, if you don't get this right."

Toby nods. Her promise seems fair enough, but the fear in her voice drives a chill through his soul. Maybe he really doesn't want to know what she knows. He takes a deep breath and focuses. "Okay," he says. "I'll do my best."

"That's all that matters."

"So, what are the rules?"

"First rule. Most important. Fats are good. Sugars are bad," she says. "Always remember. If you don't, rule two won't matter. Rule two might not save you."

"Easy enough," says Toby with a short nod. "What's rule number two?"

Clarice grips his hands tight. "Repeat it. Repeat rule number one."

"I got it, just—"

"Repeat it!" she shouts, clamping down on his hands to the point that pain shoots up his arm.

Toby jumps back and pulls his hands free. "Christ, you didn't have to break my fingers."

"Repeat it," she says again, softer this time. "Never forget it. Never."

"Fats are good. Sugars are bad."

Clarice smiles. "Drugs take longer to get to you if they're in fats," she explains. "Sugar gets in your blood quick. Makes it harder to stop. Eat only the fats. Stay away from the sugars. No treats. No soda."

Toby pops his knuckles anxiously, one at a time. He doesn't like the thought of willfully eating drugs meant to turn his mind into mush. "What next?"

"Rule two, refund the unclean."

Toby shakes his head. "I don't understand."

Clarice pulls out a couple of Bic pens from her purse and hands one of them to him. "Refund anything that's drugged," she says. She takes the pen she kept and sticks it down her throat far enough to make her gag before she pulls it back out. "That's a refund," she says. "Suck the ink out when you're done, too. Always have to have the ink, just to be sure. Do it all in the bathroom. Quick. Quiet. And don't let them see. Never let them see. Not anyone."

"What if I can't help it? What if someone is in the bathroom?"

"Never let them see," she says gravely.

"Why not skip the meal?"

Clarice wraps her arms around her midsection and grips herself tightly. "Can't skip. Tried before. But they always watch. Always mark. Only choice is to eat and get to the bathroom quick."

"How long do I have?" he asks. "I mean, from the time I eat."

"A minute or two if they're sugars," she says. "Ten minutes or so if they're fats. Fats are good."

"Right. Sugars are bad."

"Talk to yourself when you eat," she says. "Talk over and over what you have to do. Must do. Even fats make you foggy. Fats can make you forget. They're deadly too. Can't forget that. Never forget that. Repeat the rules. Always. No matter what. Repeat that you have to refund over and over until you make it there. Otherwise you'll forget."

"I think I'll remember," Toby says, flashing a nervous smile. "I'm not a geriatric."

"No!" she says, gripping his shoulders tight. "Don't take this lightly, even in jest. No matter what happens on the outside, your inside must be strong. Has to be. If you don't listen to me, if you don't repeat the rules, after you've eaten, you won't want to get clean. You'll only want to eat more. You'll be like one of them."

Toby's mouth runs dry. He forces a swallow in a vain effort to remove the lump that's formed in his throat. "And if I turn...I mean, worst case scenario and all, can you save me?"

Clarice lets him go, and her shoulders drop. "Maybe," she said. "Probably not. It's hard to save the lost. Worked once. Once. Barely at that. But it didn't last. Didn't turn out well."

Toby sucks in another deep breath. He shuts his eyes as he feels his lungs expand, and he focuses on his breath as he slowly lets it out. His nerves are building, but this focusing technique feels like it's helping keep him together. "Okay, so I won't forget the rules. I'll keep them repeating over and over. Anything else?"

Clarice bites her lip. "One last rule," she says. "Don't brag. Don't attract attention, especially with your job title. VP is bad. Very bad. Be something else. Anything."

Toby folds his arms over his chest. "Like what?"

"Anything," she says. "VP is near the top. Be something else. Entry tech. Mail clerk. Whatever. Just play dumb. Be dumb." Clarice stops and glances at the clock once more. "We've got to go. They'll be here soon. You ready?"

"Yeah. Ready as I'll ever be."

Clarice stands up on her tip toes and kisses him on the cheek. "Okay, let's go. And be good. Always good."

CHAPTER FOUR

Toby follows Clarice down the hall in silent contemplation. He wonders what the cafeteria will be like, who will be there, and how awful it might be given Clarice's dire warnings. When they reach the elevator, Clarice hits the down button, and a question pops into his mind.

"You said something about being checked for lunch?" he asks.

Clarice doesn't answer immediately. Instead, she points down the hall to where a Freddie-look-a-like, dressed in a uniform and carrying a black baton, is exiting one of the other apartments. "I told you, everyone has to eat," she whispers. She stays quiet until the guard slithers over to and enters the next apartment. "Everyone eats," she says. "Best if they don't make you. Too much attention if they bring you down."

Toby doesn't ask for details as his imagination fills in the rest. "What now?"

"Now we go to lunch," she says. "That's it. Nothing more. Just be normal. Normal is good. Normal is quiet. When we get back, we'll talk. We'll get started."

"Hard to be normal in a place like this," he says with a laugh.

"Shh!" Clarice shoots him a glare. "This place is normal? Get it?"

The fear in her voice is all that's needed to cause Toby to shut up.

A few seconds of silence pass and the elevator has yet to arrive. "What should we talk about at lunch?" he asks.

"Stamps," she says, much to his surprise. "We talk about stamps. It's the job everyone was assigned this morning. Our job. Have to make better stamps. Might have to talk about our ideas making stamps with others, too. Depends on who we sit with."

Toby looks at her with confusion. "What are you on about?"

"It's the job we were assigned," she says. "Greg talked all about it during our meeting this morning—the one you weren't there for."

"Who's Greg?"

"Boss of the department," says Clarice. "Runs the show. Well, he's the human that thinks he runs the show. Freddie obviously runs it all."

"What's our part in all of this? I mean with the stamps."

"Greg said we all had to buckle down and make a better rubber stamp. Form a committee, lead it. Come up with good ideas. Has to be a good stamp though. No, not good. Perfect. Has to be done by the end of the week."

"We're talking about rubber stamps, right? Like ones you use on paper?"

Clarice nods. "Yeah. Greg's obsessed with them. Loves them, even more than my old boss. Greg says the ones here aren't stampy enough. Wants new ones."

"I don't know the first thing about stamps," Toby admits. "I think the last one I had was in first grade, and that one had a smiley face."

"Doesn't matter. Doesn't matter," she says. "Season is tomorrow. Season will change everything. But we still have to talk about stamps. Still have to do our job till then."

The elevator dings. The doors open, and Toby soon finds himself inside, riding it down to the second floor. The air between them is silent and uncomfortable. It's the perfect sort of silence that lets his brain build question after question until he can't take it anymore.

"We're going to the cafeteria?" he asks.

"We are."

"And they want us to eat."

"They do. All of us."

"And all the food is—"

He doesn't even get the word "drugged" out before she shoves him into the wall and presses her lips against his. He's so shocked at her actions, he can't move.

When she pulls back, carnal desire is not what's on her face, despite its red hue. All that's there is a mountain of burning anger, and it's all directed at him. "Don't you listen?" she scolds in a whisper. "You have to listen to me, Toby!"

"We're alone!" he shoots back.

The elevator stops, and Toby looks up and notices it's not the second floor they've stopped at, but the third. The doors slide open, and Clarice instantly ducks behind Toby and snakes her arm around his waist. He's about to say something to her but stops when yet another Freddie-ish guard slithers in the elevator.

"You persies okay?" he says, hunching over slightly and scratching Toby under the chin. "What was that ruckus?"

Toby stares at the alien, wondering what he should say since he's certain it didn't happen to arrive in their elevator due to coincidence. As such, all he can manage is a feeble denial of everything. "What ruckus?"

"I was in my office, and I heard a ruckus."

"Could you describe the ruckus?" says Toby, still hoping that ignorance will prove to be the best policy.

Clarice eases around Toby's side. "He was complaining about the food," she says.

Toby turns and stares with an open mouth. Part of him wonders if she's going to sell him out, and the other part wonders if he should sell her out first.

Clarice turns to Toby for a moment and kisses his cheek. "It's okay, honey," she says. "He'll tell you the same thing I did."

"What's the problem with the food?" asks the guard, inching forward.

Clarice answers before Toby, which is a good thing, because he can't think of anything remotely good to say. "He's afraid it's all cold," she says. "He doesn't believe me that there's hot stuff, too."

"Silly persie," the guard says, easing back. "Of course we have hot food. Is that why you're being so cranky? Afraid you won't get something to warm that belly of yours?"

Toby lets his shoulders drop, and he tries to look as sincere as possible. "Yeah. Something like that."

"Today for lunch we have subs," the guard says, patting Toby on the head with his tail. "Do you like subs? There are hot and cold ones, I promise. And great desserts, too."

"Subs are good," Toby replies. "And I like dessert."

"Good boy," says the guard. "Tell you what," he goes on. "I'll see you two to the cafeteria, make sure you get there alright.

Wouldn't want you guys to get lost in such a big place, would we?"

"Thank you," says Clarice. She elbows Toby in the ribs.

"Ow," he says, rubbing his side. After seeing her glance to the guard, he quickly tacks on. "And, uh, thanks."

The guard pushes the button for the second floor, and the doors close behind him. The guard keeps his back to Toby and Clarice, and though he's not watching them with his eyes, Toby is certain he's under close scrutiny.

"So, how about them stamps," Toby says.

"Need to make more," says Clarice. "Lots more."

The elevator resumes its decent, and that's all the conversation Toby can muster. Anything he thinks to say or do seems silly and so obviously fabricated that he stands in silence with his breath held. Sweat beads on his neck and trickles down his back. He studies the guard's every move. He catches sight of the alien twitching its left hand for a split second. Toby's brain goes into overdrive as it tries to decipher the meaning behind the movement. Is it signaling an attack? Was the guard about to swing on them with its baton? Pepper Spray? Hidden tranquilizer? Or worse? Maybe it just had an itch to scratch. It is, after all, stifling hot inside the elevator, Toby decides. And just how damn long does it take to go from the third floor to the second anyway?

Toby looks to Clarice, hoping for some silent input on the guard dilemma. But the moment he does, the elevator comes to a halt and the doors open with a ding.

"Here we go, persies," says the guard, slithering out. "Let's get those bellies of yours nice and full with yummy treats."

"Come on, Toby," Clarice says, pulling him forward by is forearm. "You're hungry, aren't you? Must be. Should be."

"I'm hungry," says Toby. The guard's ever watchful gaze raises goose bumps on his arms. "Always hungry," Toby then adds, trying to mimic Clarice as best he can. "Always ready to eat some more."

"Good boy," the guard says, patting Toby on the head. "Now follow me."

All three of them proceed down the hall, taking three corners and passing by two cubicle farms, with Clarice remaining latched onto Toby's side the entire time.

"Here we are," the guard says, once they arrive at the cafeteria's steel double doors. "Enjoy!"

Toby says nothing, and he quickly goes inside with Clarice right behind. He halts the instant he enters, and Clarice bounces off his back. "Wow," is all he can say.

"What?" asks Clarice.

Toby doesn't answer. His senses are too busy trying to recover from the massive overload they've taken in. Warm lights, brick and wood paneled walls, and decked out serving bars make him feel like he's stepped into the dining area of a five-star restaurant in a Vegas casino. The assault on his nose from the aroma of spices, cheeses, and sauces of all kinds make him want to eat and never stop. And last but not least, the sounds of loud laughter and conversation that fill his ears makes him want to be included in whatever party is going on.

"This," he finally says, eyes wide. "This isn't right."

"What's not?" she says. Her voice sounds wary, more so than usual.

"The cafeteria back at—" he starts to say, but quickly stops himself when he realizes he's about to break a cardinal rule: no talking about home. So, he quickly redacts his comment. "I didn't expect such a great place to eat is all."

"They want us to eat," says Clarice. "They want us to enjoy it."

"Yeah, I can see that."

Clarice grabs him by the shoulders and points him toward the food. Two separate buffets sit at either side of the serving area which is about twenty feet away. To the left is an assortment of wrapped sandwiches, subs, and gyros, with a salad bar tacked on to the end. To the right is tray after tray of deserts, from ice cream to apple pie to pastry delights. Toby's stomach rumbles at the sight of it all.

"Don't forget number one," Clarice whispers as she pulls him along.

"I haven't," Toby says.

"I mean it."

"I know," says Toby as they file behind the other coworkers waiting for their turn at the buffet. The line moves fast, and before he knows it, he's seated at a booth in the back of the dining area with Clarice sitting across from him. He stares down at his food—a foot-long meatball sub and a tall glass of milk— and hopes he got what he was supposed to. "I...I wasn't sure what was good here," he says, picking his words as carefully as he can. "So, I got what you did."

Clarice takes a drink from her milk and wipes away her new mustache with a paper napkin. "You're fine. Bathrooms are to the left if you have to pee."

Toby glances over and finds them without any trouble. He's about to turn to Clarice once more when he spots a group of coworkers all gathered around a circular table being especially loud and boisterous. From their expressions and gestures, he guesses they're having some sort of party. He watches for a moment until a cake, covered in white icing and trimmed in pink, is brought out and set before a woman who's in the center of it all.

"Birthday?" Toby asks.

"Not a birthday," Clarice replies. "Baby shower. Lexi's baby shower. You can tell because she's tagged."

Toby spies the tag in an instant. It's hanging from her left ear, large and pink, and it reminds him of the ones he's seen on nature shows.

"Why tag her if she's pregnant?" he asks.

"Makes Lexi special," Clarice says. "Let's everyone know to treat her nice."

"But I thought..." Toby catches himself before he goes any further. He spends a second rephrasing his question in the hopes that it doesn't alert any eavesdroppers while still keeping it comprehensible to Clarice. "Special is good?"

"Pink tags are always good," she replies. "Especially since she's a board member. Means she'll probably be chairman next season, too."

"What about you?"

"I'm not a board member. I'm a lowly secretary. Can't be chairman. Which is fine, really. I don't want anything else."

"No," says Toby. "I mean, have you ever been tagged?"

"You mean pregnant?"

"Yeah," he says with a stifled laugh. "Wasn't sure if that was something I could ask. Or even should, I guess."

"No, not yet," she says. "Been trying. Been trying for a long time. Was hoping you could make that happen."

Toby looks down, unsure if she's being serious or if it's part of an act she's playing. Either way, he doesn't know how to respond.

"Eat," she whispers.

Toby looks up.

"Eat. Eat now. Fast." she says, chowing down on her sub. "Eat and repeat. Always repeat what I told you."

Toby looks around the cafeteria, and it's not long before he realizes what the source of Clarice's concern is. Freddie is escorting a group of aliens around the dining area, ten in all, each dressed in a business suit that looks like it came from The

Aliens Warehouse. And if it weren't for the pith helmets atop their heads, they would look like any other coworker, though better dressed—alien origins aside.

The group snakes its way around the tables, stopping every now and then to talk to the people nearby. Toby watches, riveted, and he's dying to know what this is all about.

Before he has a chance to figure it out, a cacophony comes from the serving line and snatches his attention. Aliens, six of them in all, come running into the dining area, yelling and screeching. Two of them are dressed similar to the group that Freddie is escorting, but the other four are wearing poorly made, rubber human suits and are splattered with red paint.

The half-dozen aliens quickly form a circle in the middle of the dining hall and turn their screeching into a rhythmic chant. Toby has no idea what they're saying, but the entire lot makes him think they've recently escaped a Far Side cartoon.

Toby throws a glance to Freddie who looks thoroughly irritated. Freddie doesn't say anything, but simply shakes his head and whips out a little gray box about the size of a small stack of business cards and talks into it.

Within moments, two dozen aliens flood the cafeteria and it's clear they mean business. Each has a baton in hand and slick-looking armor plates covering their chest and legs. These new arrivals club the pseudo-humans and faux businessmen like baby seals before binding them with ties and dragging them away.

Once they're gone, only a few heartbeats pass before the dining room returns to normal. People go back to eating and Freddie returns to schmoozing with his alien party.

"What was that?" Toby asks, eyes still fixed on where it all went down.

"Stop looking," Clarice answers. "It's not important."

Toby obeys. Sort of. Though he turns around, he can't shake the event from his mind. He has to know. "Seriously," he whispers. "What happened?"

Clarice bites her knuckle and glances around the room. Her voice drops so low Toby can barely make out her words. "They come from time to time," she says. "Come to disrupt. They come to...come to protest."

She doesn't even say the last word. Toby has to do his best to read her lips to get it.

Toby mouths his reply. "Protest what?"

"Go back to eating," she says, sipping her milk. "We've got to finish. Got to stick to the rules."

Toby sighs. He's not getting any more answers out of her while they're here. That much is clear. Maybe when they're in a more private place she'll fill him in, so he decides he might as well eat and get it over with.

Toby picks up his sub and repeats her rules in his head. Fats are good. Sugars are bad. Refund the unclean.

He takes a deep breath and prepares to chow down. He wonders what this will be like and whether he'll survive the drugs designed to turn his brain into mush.

Clarice seems to have, sort of. And he doesn't have much of a choice, either. He can feel them watching his every move—the aliens, his coworkers, and the rest of them. They are all watching and waiting to see if he's become the good employee they expect him to be.

It's either that or Clarice's paranoia is rubbing off on him.

Then again, it's not paranoia if it's true.

"So, have you two bumped uglies yet?"

Toby spins around to see Matt pull a chair over to the end of their table and plop down in it. He then sets his tray that's complete with gyro and orange juice at his spot.

Toby waits a moment for Clarice to reply, but when she doesn't, he feels pressured to say something. "We've been, um, working on a new project."

"Dude, right, that stamp thing," Matt replies. "Wanted to talk to you about that, actually."

"You did?" asks Toby, putting his sub down.

"Totally," he says. "I don't think it's fair you get such a righteous nameplate when I have Kay."

Toby's face is hit by a massive ball of confusion. "What are you talking about?"

"Dude, nameplates? Titles?" says Matt, eyebrows arched. He leans back a little and crosses his arms over his chest. "Stop being a peal. You know what I'm talking about."

"Right, titles," says Toby, still not following but not wanting to antagonize the surfer. All he wants is for the guy to go. "What about them?"

"You've got massive letters, brah," says Matt. "'Vice President of Communications and Investment Opportunities for the Acquisition of Hostile Companies,' has ninety of them. I counted. Mine's only eighty. That ain't right."

Toby's clueless expression doesn't change. He glances over to Clarice for help. But when she only shrugs, he takes the best guess he can. "You're jealous at the length of my name tag?"

Matt shakes his head as he finishes off his juice. "Just saying that's not right, dude."

"Why's that?"

Matt tears off a bit of a paper napkin, balls it, and throws it at Toby's head. "I said stop being such a peal, dude. Bigger name tag, bigger prestige. That's like asking why you'd rather ride a fat wave instead of an ankle snapper."

Toby shrugs, indifferent to Matt's assertion. "I was over you before, you know," he says. "What's the big deal if I'm over you now?"

"I've got three secretaries," he says. "That's what."

"You've only got one right now," Toby corrects.

"Well, I will have three once Freddie ponies up."

Toby raises an eyebrow. "So you're saying because you have three secretaries, you think you should have a longer tag than me?"

"Exactly. I'm clearly better than you. Kay's a bunny—my bunny. All you've got is Clarice. She looks like she wiped in some coral coming off the bomb."

Toby balls a fist at his side, under the table. He's not about to punch Matt over mere words, but he likes to imagine smashing the kid's nose across his face for saying something so mean.

"I've got to go," Clarice says. To Toby's surprise, she seems indifferent to the entire conversation.

"You okay?" he asks.

"I'm fine," she replies. "Bathroom and all. Have to go."

"Ciao," says Matt. When she passes by, he grabs her arm. "My bad. Didn't mean anything by that last thing."

Clarice pulls away. "I know," she says. She then looks over to Toby. "Eat. Come back to my place. Need to talk. Want to talk."

Matt watches her leave and when she disappears into the women's restroom, he turns back around and says, "Even if you bag her tonight, that doesn't change anything. I still deserve a better tag than you."

"I honestly don't care who has what name tag," says Toby. "Besides, I didn't give myself the job. Freddie did. Remember? Maybe you should take it up with him."

"Dude! You're right," Matt says, shaking his head and laughing. "Totally my bad, brah. Here I am thinking you hacked me, and it wasn't your fault at all. Let's get the Big Kahuna in on this." Matt twists around and eyeballs Freddie's group until the alien happens to look his way. When he does, Matt waves him over.

"Freddie," Matt says once the alien arrives. "I've got a humungous problem here. Like, worse than a beach full of whales with butt floss."

Though Matt is talking to Freddie, the alien's gaze isn't on Matt. It falls on Toby's plate—Toby's full plate of untouched food to be more precise. "What's the matter, persie?" Freddie asks. "Not hungry?"

Toby stiffens at the unexpected observation. His mouth runs dry as Clarice's warnings run rampant through his mind. "No, no. I got distracted," Toby says. He grabs the sub, takes a big bite, and washes it down with a gulp of milk. "It's good."

Warmth builds in Toby's stomach. Not as fast or as hard as it had with the Rice Krispy Treats, but it's there, nonetheless. His senses start to dull, as if he's had his first big swig of triple-bock beer on an empty stomach.

"I knew you'd be happy here," Freddie says.

"Well, the food is delicious," says Toby, taking another bite. The warmth in his belly spreads through his torso and runs down his limbs. The tips of his fingers tingle, and the milk he drinks no longer quenches his thirst. He wants an ice-cold Sprite, and he flirts with the idea of getting up for one.

"What seems to be the problem?" asks Freddie.

Toby stops eating and considers the question. Sure, he doesn't care for the atmosphere in the cafeteria all that much, but it's nothing to have a meltdown over, especially when a little mood music and better lighting would do the trick. So as far as he's concerned, things are peachy keen.

"I'll tell you what the problem is, boss," Matt says. "Toby here has ninety letters to his name plate, and I only have eighty. Not cool at all."

"Aw, silly persie," Freddie says, patting Matt on the head. "We can't give everyone long name tags."

"I'm not everyone," protests Matt. "I'm nailing Kay, aren't I? You're getting me two more secretaries, aren't you? Even if they aren't Emmas, three secs makes me badass. More badass than Toby for sure. He's only got Clarice. And my office is totally gnarly. His isn't heinous or anything, but it ain't all that."

Clarice? Toby stops chewing at the mention of her name. There's something about her he was supposed to remember. Something important. He closes his eyes, tries to think. In his mind, he can see her staring at him, telling him to never forget. Don't forget what? Don't forget to turn off the lights? Don't forget to file the TPS reports? Try as he might, Toby can't come up with anything.

"You know, you're right," says Freddie, cutting into Toby's thoughts. "You've been very assertive in climbing the corporate ladder. I like that. My guests really like that. Let's correct that right now. Does that sound good?"

"That sounds totally rad!" Matt says with a fist pump.

Toby wants to get up, get another sub, and trade his milk in for a soda, but when Freddie whips out a little box-shaped device, he stays seated in the booth and figures something is about to happen that he doesn't want to miss. For a few seconds, he watches Freddie fiddle with the device. It's apparently not cooperating with Freddie whatsoever, for the alien taps it a few times on the table before he looks up at Matt.

"What's your job title, again?" Freddie asks.

"Vice President of Marketing and Development of Strategic Positions in Volatile Environments," answers Matt.

Freddie taps his box a few more times until it beeps. "There we go," he says. "So, let's make you the Executive Vice President of All Marketing and Development of Strategic Positions in Volatile Environments. That's ninety-two letters long."

"Sweet."

"Best make the announcement now," Freddie says. "All of our guests will be eager to know as well, and I hate to have to repeat myself."

Repeat? Toby knows that word. It's a special word. He runs his fingers through his hair, digs his nails into his scalp. Repeat something. Repeat what?

Matt taps him on the shoulder. "Hey brah," he says. "Just so you know, if Clarice wants to bail and come back to me, I'll make her stay with you."

"Huh?" says Toby.

"Just saying, if she bails on you for me, name tag and all, I'll tell her she works for you," Matt replies as he leans back in his chair. "It's the least I can do."

"Oh god, Clarice," Toby says.

"But I don't think she'll really bail on you, dude. No worries."

Toby shakes his head as her warnings about this place, the food, and the dire need to empty his stomach and suck down ink come flooding back. But even with that revelation, his mind continues to fog, and holding on to those warnings is near impossible.

Thankfully, Toby still has enough wits left to realize he's losing it. He knows he has to reach a bathroom posthaste. His hand reaches into his pocket. A small bit of relief washes over him. His salvation, the Bic pen, is still there.

As Toby stands and excuses himself, the lights go out, and a spotlight falls on Freddie. He's a dozen feet away, standing in the middle of the room, holding a microphone.

"Good evening, patrons and persies from far and wide," Freddie says. "I hope you all are having a wonderful last lunch before the start of a new and exciting season."

Numerous cheers and claps fill the room, and Freddie basks in the praise, bowing, and waving in a half dozen different directions.

Toby inches away as he heads for the bathroom. Must refund. Must purge. Must be clean. His eyes haven't adjusted to the dark, but he thinks he can see well enough to not bump into anyone or anything and avoid an incident.

He gets a few steps toward his goal when a second spot light falls directly on him, and he realizes he's not going anywhere.

CHAPTER FIVE

Toby freezes like a deer caught in headlights. He knows he can't bolt for the bathroom, but he also knows he has to do something to ward off the drugs, so he does the first thing that comes to mind. He drives one foot into the ground so that the same two toes he injured in Clarice's apartment scream in agony. His eyes water, and it's all he can do not to cry. But he can think clearer now.

"I have an announcement," Freddie says, beaming at Toby and Matt. "I'd like to announce a promotion! Our dear friend Matt is now the Executive Vice President of All Marketing and Development of Strategic Positions in Volatile Environments, effective immediately!"

Applause, shouts, and whistles fill the room. Calls for a speech follow. Freddie raises all three of his hands and bids the crowd to be quiet. Once the room's volume drops twenty decibels, he waves Matt over. "Why don't you come say a few words?"

"Wow, dude," Matt says stumbling with his reply. "I don't know where to start."

"Start by taking the microphone," says Freddie, offering it to the surfer.

The unseen crowd erupts in laughter.

Matt jumps out of his chair and hurries over. The spotlight follows, and once again, Toby is in the dark.

"Go, Toby. Go," he says to himself. He darts to the bathroom and manages to avoid most of the obstacles along the way. He does bump into a few people, but thankfully his quick apologizes smooth over any transgressions.

Toby reaches the men's room and yanks the door open by its cold, steel handle. Bright, white light pours out, and Toby shields his eyes momentarily as he enters. Small tiles on the floor gleam under the fluorescent bulbs above. The air smells of disinfectant, and Toby is impressed at how clean the place looks.

Toby hurries past the sinks and mirror on his left, past the three urinals on the same side, and opens the first of two stall doors. Wrapped around the toilet seat is black and yellow caution tape, and there's a sign above that says, "Out of order."

"Gah!" says Toby, moving on to the next stall. His mind clouds again, and he drives his battered toes into the wall. The fire that races through his foot and leg is a welcomed one and clarity returns.

Toby tries to open the second stall, but it's locked.

"Someone is in here," a voice says.

Toby instantly recognizes the voice. It belongs to Boris, and that's a guy he'll never forget no matter how many drugs are pumping through his body.

"You wait till I am done," Boris tacks on.

"Sorry," says Toby, instinctively backing up. He paces around the bathroom and tries to convince himself it won't be long. Judging by Boris's constant grunts, strains, and distinct lack of splashing sounds, Toby thinks otherwise.

Toby considers using the urinals or the broken toilet in the other stall to puke his guts into, but figures the foremost would be bad to use if someone walked in, and the latter would leave evidence behind. And that, he decides, can't be good. He doesn't want to explain things to Freddie.

Toby repeats the first two rules in his head, over and over. Fat is good. Sugar is bad. Refund the unclean. As the pain in his foot subsides, his concentration wanes. The rules become harder and harder to repeat.

"Fat is sugar. Refund the un-good," Toby mumbles. He shakes his head, grits his teeth. "Think Toby," he says. "Think. Think. Think."

The rules in his mind turn vague. He knows they're important, but he can't remember what they are. He does remember, however, that pain seems to bring them back. Pain can help. Pain does help. Toby kicks his foot against the wall again, and it offers a brief respite from the drug's effects.

"Fats are good. Sugars are bad. Refund the unclean," he whispers with a bright smile. He's back. He prays it will last. But it doesn't. A few repeats later, all Toby can say to himself is, "Refund the unclean."

Toby paces for what feels like an eternity. The drugs claw at his mind, so he kicks the wall again with his foot, only this time, it barely helps.

Desperate, Toby stumbles into the empty stall and drops to his knees. The tile floor does a number on his knee caps, which is enough to buy him a few more moments of clarity.

Toby whips out his Bic pen, shoves it down his throat, and pukes. Bits of partially digested sub spew out of his mouth. Most of it goes in the toilet, but some splatters on the floor.

He then snaps the pen in half and sucks down the ink for all he's worth. The bitter liquid coats his tongue and makes bile rise in his throat. He pants for a few moments, and as his concentration returns, he smiles.

Toby stumbles getting to his feet. He leans against the wall before spitting into the toilet. "Jesus," he mutters. "That's nasty."

The toilet in the other stall flushes, and Toby hears Boris call out. "What you say is nasty?"

"Nothing," Toby replies. In a panic, he tries the handle. Nothing happens. The remains of his lunch float in the bowl, a telltale sign to his deception. Toby backs out of the stall and closes the door just as Boris comes out of his.

"It sound like you sick," Boris says, eyeing Toby suspiciously. "Maybe you need trip to infirmary, yes? Maybe I take you there to make sure you have not contaminated whole office."

Toby holds his hands up and steps back a few. "No, no," he says, talking as fast as he can. "That's won't be necessary. I'm a little overwhelmed is all."

"Coward like you, is not surprising."

"Right. That stamp committee, you know, has me worked up," Toby says.

"No, I do not know about stamp committee. What is this you're talking about?"

"Stamps," Toby says, trying to remember anything and everything Clarice had said on the matter. "We're making new ones. Designer stamps for the professional businessman on the go. It's really important."

"I would know if something is important," Boris counters. "I would be told to protect such a thing."

"Right, well, the project starts tomorrow, so that's when Freddie was going to tell you," Toby replies. Despite the plausibility of the lie, Toby prays Boris won't check up on it for a while. It'll never hold under scrutiny.

"You say these are designer stamps?"

"Yeah. Why?"

"Designer stamps sound like something medals given for to keep safe."

Toby shrugs. Medals being handed out in the corporate world are nothing he's ever considered, let alone heard of, but then again, this place is anything but normal. "Probably," he finally answers. "With some luck, we'll all get one for doing a good job."

"You say you want medals?" he asks, advancing on Toby. "You say because you know my Melissa likes medals, don't you?"

"Seriously," Toby says hands back up defensively. "I'm not after your girl."

"You think I'm stupid?" Boris says, advancing. "That you think I don't know how beautiful she is?"

"No—"

"Then you say she is ugly?"

"No!" Toby says. It's a little more forceful than he intended, and as soon as he says it, he gives a quick prayer that the steroid popping freak in front of him doesn't charge.

Boris doesn't. Not yet, at least. He narrows his eyes and one hand drifts to the gun on his belt. "Then what are you saying?"

"All I'm saying is that maybe they'll give medals," Toby replies, backing up until the hot air blower on the wall is digging into his side. "You can have all the medals if you want. You've probably earned them."

Boris stays where he is, folds his arms, and grunts. "You better not be trying to trick me," he says.

"I'm not. I swear."

"Then I go talk to Melissa," he says. "She will be excited to hear I get new medals."

Boris leaves without further word, and Toby falls back against the wall with a great exhale. His mouth still feels slimy and nasty, and he briefly considers rinsing it out. Ultimately, he decides against it. He needs to get away from the scene of his crime and get back to Clarice's apartment. There, they can get this escape plan of hers underway, not to mention he can always rinse his mouth out at her place as well.

Toby cracks the exit door open and looks out. Freddie is nowhere in sight. Neither is Matt or anyone else he knows. He slips out of the bathroom and hugs the wall as he moves through the dining area.

He's about to make it out of the cafeteria when a tap on his shoulder roots him in place. Toby spins around and standing a few feet away is a female Mr. Squid— a Mrs. Squid. Or maybe it's Miss. Or Ms.

Regardless of the prefix, Toby is reasonably sure it's a girl since she's dressed in a white shirt with a light pink jacket, and slick, feminine looking black pants. In her tentacles she's holding a small book with Preser Tech's logo printed across the front.

"Who-oo are you-oo?" she asks in a light, melodic voice. Her vowels draw out a good one or two seconds longer than Toby is used to, and it gives Toby an extra helping of the willies.

"Toby," he replies. He's not sure if Clarice would've wanted him to be truthful, but she had warned him not to draw attention, and getting caught in a lie right now would no doubt do exactly that.

"Toe-oo-bee?" she says, flipping through the book and periodically glancing up at him.

Curiosity latches on to Toby like a lion taking down a gazelle. As much as he wants to leave, he can't. He has to know what she's looking at. Toby takes a tentative step forward and takes a peek.

The book she's reading is filled with pictures, all of them headshots of office workers. Though Toby doesn't recognize any of the faces in the book, and despite the fact he can't even begin to read the alien writing contained therein, he guesses she's flipping through a yearbook or corporate directory of some sort.

"Where is Toe-oo-bee?" she says, handing him the book.

Toby looks at what she's offering but doesn't take it. "I don't think I'm in there," he says. "I'm new."

"Ne-ew?" Mrs. Squid says. She flips through the pages, front to back, back to front, searching for something. On her third trip through, a small leaflet drops out and flutters to the ground. On it are six more headshots, one of them being Toby's. Mrs. Squid picks the leaflet up and points to Toby's picture. "Toe-oo-bee?"

Toby squints. Sure enough, that's him. He has no idea when and where the picture was taken. He doesn't remember having it done at all. But there's no denying that's him. "Yes, that's me," he says.

"Toe-oo-bee Ree-sha-ard Ben-net," she says.

"Right. Toby Richard Bennet," Toby says with a sigh. If there's any reason for her not to know his full name, it doesn't matter now.

"Toe-oo-bee is Vee-Pee?" she asks.

Against his screaming intuition, Toby answers the question as he figures she already knows the answer. "Yeah. Why?" he says.

Mrs. Squid doesn't answer. She lets out a bubbling noise and using a red pen, circles Toby's picture several times over before furiously scribbling a few notes in the margin.

"Bye, Toe-oo-Bee," she says, patting him on the head. "Stay big."

Mrs. Squid leaves, and Toby stands still for a moment as he tries to figure out what happened, but he comes up with nothing. Thus, he scoots out of the cafeteria and gets on the elevator.

He stares at the buttons, and his heart sinks. He's not sure where Clarice's apartment is. Eleventh floor, maybe? He decides to give it a go and hits the button. The elevator whisks him up, and Toby prays it doesn't stop until it's reached his floor.

The doors open on the eleventh floor, and Toby steps out. The hall looks familiar, save for the fact that there's a water fountain down on one end that he doesn't remember being there. But there's also an alien nearby, stooped over and working on it, so Toby decides maybe it's being freshly installed.

Toby heads to the right, toward the general area he thinks Clarice's apartment is, all the while, he studies each apartment number as it goes by, hoping one will jog his memory. When that effort proves futile, he knocks softly on the first door on his left.

"Clarice?" he says. When no one answers, he knocks again and then moves on.

It takes four more tries, each at a separate apartment, before the door he's waiting at opens. To his relief, Clarice is on the other side and pulls him in.

"You took long," she says once she's shut the door. "Too long. Was worried. Thought you might not come back. Thought you'd leave me too."

"I'm not leaving you," Toby says. "Not as long as you can get us out."

Clarice wraps herself up in her arms and rocks on her heels. "Always said that. Always. But it doesn't change. He's gone now. Gone."

"I'm not leaving," Toby states with force. Hopefully, it will settle the matter. "You're the only one helping me."

"Okay, okay, okay." Clarice breathes deep. A smile, clearly forced, spreads on her face. "You're staying. I believe you. Really."

Toby gives a smile of his own. "Good. Besides, you're the one that left me, remember?" He tacks on a laugh at the end and hopes she doesn't take it the wrong way.

"Had to leave. Had to," she says. "Had to refund. Had to purge the unclean. Can't sit back down. Sitting down means more food. More food and no ink. Bad combination. Very bad."

"Yeah, I know," says Toby. "What do we do now?"

Clarice takes his hand and leads him over to the bed. She pushes him back until he sits. "I...I don't have a plan," she says, stumbling. "Not a new one. Just sex. Sex has to work. It must. There's no other choice."

"Clarice," Toby says, tone lowering. "I'm not sleeping with you. So if this is some sort of game—"

"Not a game, not a game," Clarice says. She grabs his hands and holds them tight. "I can't think of anything else. Please. You have to have screw me. Have to."

"No."

"You'll like it, I promise," she says, not letting him pull his hands back. "We'll be good together. Good mates for one another. That's what they want to see, don't you get it? We'll be special. I'll be special. That's what has to happen."

Toby instantly takes to his feet. "I knew it," he says, anger building. He scolds himself for trusting her when she's clearly as cracked as the rest. "You only want to get knocked up so you can get one of those pink tags, right? You're as bat shit crazy as everyone else."

Clarice jumps back and crouches, hands out. "No, no, no," she spits out. "No sex. Fine. Fine. I was hoping, is all. I was hoping you'd changed your mind. But you won't. You won't. I still want to get out. I still need your help."

Toby crosses his arms, forces himself to give her the benefit of the doubt, for the next sixty seconds at least. "You said we need one of their keys, right?"

Clarice nods.

"Then think, Clarice," he says. "How do we get their keys? Can we take one of them down?"

Clarice falls back against the wall and sinks to the floor. "No. Can't do that. Too strong. Too many of them will come and come fast."

"You know this place," says Toby. "What else can we try?"

Clarice buries her face in her hands. "I don't know."

Toby looks at her with sympathy. He's still wary at her insatiable desire to breed, but he's also convinced that she wants to get out. As such, Toby sits back on the bed with a sigh and hopes they can come up with something viable. "What are our assets?" he asks.

"Not much," she says, face still buried. "We don't have much here. Only what you see around. And in the office. Have some paper there. And pens. But those won't open portals. Those won't help us escape."

Toby looks around the apartment until his gaze falls on some clothes Clarice has on the floor. He squints for a moment until he realizes one of the pants she has tucked in the corner are a pair of black parachute pants from 80s. "God, those are old," he mutters. "Can't remember the last time I saw those."

Clarice glances over to what he's looking at. "Most things are," she says. "New is rare. New is fought over. I don't get new things. Don't want them either. Makes you stand out."

"How long have you been here?" asks Toby.

Clarice slowly shakes her head but doesn't say a word.

Toby takes a deep breath and exhales sharply. "Well, that's one thing we got then, and plenty of."

"What's that?" she asks.

"Time," Toby says with a grin. "Lots and lots of time."

The look on Clarice's face says she's not sharing his attempt at humor. "No, no time," she says. "No time at all."

"What do you mean?"

Clarice stares off to the side. Her eyes widen, and her face drains of color. "No time to waste, Clarice," she whispers. "Has to be now. Has to. Has to. Just hold still. Hold still and it will all be over."

Worried, Toby leans over and puts his hands on her shoulders. "You okay?"

Clarice snaps back and hits her head on the wall. The shock seems enough to bring her back to the present. "Need more time to prepare," she says, digging her nails into her arms. "More time. More. We're not ready for tomorrow."

Toby keeps his eyes locked with hers. "Okay," he says, gently taking her hands in his. "We'll get more time." He's not sure what she means, but as she relaxes at his words and his touch, he decides that must be a good thing. "How do we do get more time?"

Clarice pulls away and rocks. "There's a way. But only one way. But two is better than one, and one is better than gone." She starts to hyperventilate and spends a few moments struggling for control. "I can get us more time," she finally says.

"Then do it."

"You won't like it," she replies. She drags her nails across her arms, drawing blood in the process. "Oh god, it hurts. But we'll survive. We'll make it."

"Clarice!" says Toby, grabbing her attention once more. "I need you to hold it together."

Clarice shudders, shakes her head. "I'm sorry," she says. "I'm trying. I'm trying, really."

She looks away, but Toby is quick to take her chin in his hand and turn her face toward his. "Listen to me, Clarice," he says, softly but firmly. "We're getting out of here. Now get with it. If you have to do something to get us more time so we can escape, then do it. Do whatever the hell you have to do as long as it means we get out of here alive, okay?"

Clarice bites her lower lip and pushes herself up and onto her feet. "Okay. Okay. Okay. You're right. I can do that. Will do that. You wait here, and I'll go. Might take a while, though. So stay put."

"I'm not going anywhere."

"Be sure you don't," she says, wiping her eyes. "Watch TV. That will be good. You don't want to get caught in the halls. Trust me on that."

"If it's not safe, then why are you going out there?"

"Safer for me than you," she says. "Much safer."

"What exactly are you going to do?" he asks.

"Don't ask," she says. "Best you don't know, because you don't want to. But it'll help. Please remember that. Always remember that. I'm only going to help us, save us."

With that, Clarice slips out the apartment, and Toby considers her words. She's a total crackpot, but then again, who wouldn't be after spending even a week in here?

Not wanting to think about their predicament any further, Toby grabs the remote from the night stand and props himself up in bed with a few pillows.

As he lays there thinking, he gets a whiff of the perfume that's sitting on the dresser across the room. Blood diverts to his groin, and it takes considerable mental fortitude for Toby to push away his animal urges and flip on the TV when he knows the bathroom is a few paces away.

Chocolate bars dance across the screen, and a catchy jingle plays in the background. Toby's mouth salivates. His stomach rumbles. The commercial ends, and Toby absently flips the channel. It lands on a station playing Star Wars: A New Hope.

Toby settles in bed. He's always liked this movie, and even if he's seen it a hundred times before, he's more than willing to see it a hundred times again. He watches the screen as the Millennium Falcon gets pulled into the Death Star.

"They're not going to get me without a fight," Han says on screen.

Toby yawns and gives Obi-Wan's next line in perfect unison. "You can't win. But there are alternatives to fighting."

As the battered spaceship is pulled into the Death Star and heavy music grows in his ears, Toby's eyes drop before closing altogether. Sleep quickly follows.

CHAPTER SIX

Clarice rocks inside ill-lit basement and hugs herself. The mailroom door is a few feet away, but she can't bring herself to go in. The musty air has brought back a flood of unwanted memories, and it's all she can do not to turn tail and run.

The memories are ones of her being chased through these dark and twisted basement halls, memories that end with her hiding behind a makeshift barricade inside a tucked away storage room. Deep down she knows there's more to the memories than that, but for the sake of her fragile psyche, she doesn't dare drudge up the details. She has work to do, and dwelling on the past will only cripple her for hours.

"They're not chasing you, Clarice," she whispers. "Not at all. We're safe now. Safe. The past can't hurt us, not anymore."

Clarice looks down at the manila envelope she has clutched against her chest. The papers inside are bursting from the open top. She's not sure what's written on them since they were simply a stack of notices she found in the cubicle farm and never gave them a second glance, but that's not important. She's not mailing anyone. They are merely a needed sacrifice.

Clarice gives three light raps on the door and bites one knuckle as she waits for it to open. It doesn't take long. The door cracks open about four inches, and in the darkness beyond, Clarice makes out the beady eyes of a mailroom clerk looking at her.

"What?" the man says.

"Need supplies," Clarice says. "Envelopes, labels. Things like that."

"We have none," he replies.

The clerk goes to shut the door, but Clarice, anticipating such a quick rebuff, jams her foot in the door. "There's more," she said. "Have some things that have to get mailed to HR. Important stuff. VP stuff."

The door swings open again, wider than before. The clerk steps partially out of the darkness allowing Clarice to get a better view of the man. His head is bald, and his body is hunched over so he's a good six inches shorter than he should be. Pale, pasty skin stretches tight over a thin frame, and his mouth hangs open. "You have mail?" he says, wiping away some drool.

"I do."

"Important mail?" he asks. "Very important you say?"

Clarice nods. "Very."

The clerk lunges forward with outstretched hands like a demented child lusting after his favorite toy, but Clarice jumps back before he can snatch her manila envelope from her grasp.

"Can't leave without supplies," she says. "Labels. More envelopes."

The clerk growls and spins around twice in place. Clarice isn't sure whether or not he'll let her in, but she's certain he's contemplating that very question.

The clerk glances left, right, and then behind Clarice, apparently searching the shadows for others. When he seems convinced that Clarice is alone, he says, "Fine, fine. Must see how busy we are, yes? Must ask the others if we can help."

The clerk steps back in the mailroom, swings the door wide, and ushers Clarice in. "Come, come," he says. "Show them what you've brought."

Clarice enters. The mailroom is as she remembers, stretching a good twenty feet in either direction and about half of that in depth. A pair of single-bulb lights hang from the ceiling, offering the barest of illumination. A half-dozen, flimsy, plastic desks are scattered around. Mail clerks sit at five of them, each one a runt of a man, bent over and twisted. Each one looks at Clarice with hunger in his eyes.

"She brings mail," says the clerk who let her in. "Mail that's important. Must go out, she says."

A chair scrapes across the floor to her left, and Clarice whips around. One of the other clerks scoots out from behind his desk and scampers over. "What have you?" he asks.

"Forms from our VP," Clarice answers, clutching her folder. "Evaluations for HR. Some check items for payroll."

More chairs scrape in the darkness, and a moment later, Clarice is surrounded by all of them ne. They look at one another expectantly. One even steps forward only to be grabbed by the shoulders by two others and yanked back. Their panting echoes loudly in her ears. The sight of their open, drooling mouths makes her wish she hadn't come.

"She taunts us," says one.

"She wants the mail for herself," says another.

Clarice shakes her head, and she spins in place, feeling like a deer trapped by wolves. "No, no," she says. "I only want supplies."

"Take, take, take," says a third. "Our mailroom. Our rules."

A hand grabs her arm and yanks her sideways. Clarice struggles to keep her balance and manages to do so until two more clerks pile on.

Clarice drops to her knees. At first, she protects her paper-stuffed envelope as best she can. Then, summoning the last bit of strength in her legs, she pushes herself up long enough to launch the envelop into the air.

It sails across the room, through the beam of light provided by one of the room's bulbs and hits the floor in the darkness beyond. Immediately, the clerks race after it, grabbing, pulling, and snapping at one another. They pounce on the pack of papers, tear it apart, and stuff their mouths with the torn pages.

Clarice takes to her feet and backs away. For a span of several breaths, she can't help but watch the feeding frenzy. Then her brain restarts and kicks her into gear. "No time to watch," she whispers. "Have to go. Have to get what we came for."

Clarice nods to herself and runs to the other end of the mailroom. There's a small, winding hall here that leads her past several storage rooms. She skips the first four doors and enters the fifth with bated breath.

Without looking, Clarice reaches to her right and flips the switch on the wall. She's only been here once, but she'll never forget the layout. The room is tightly packed with boxes along the walls that are filled with reams of paper. At the far end stands a set of plastic shelves, bolted to the wall, and holding countless manila envelopes.

Clarice closes the door behind her. It shuts with a click and sends a shiver up her spine. The walls close in, and her breathing turns shallow and quick.

"We're okay," she whispers, trying to steady herself. "We're okay. We're okay. Just in and out."

Her words fail to comfort her, and Clarice knows she won't last long. It's only a matter of time before the clerks find her, or worse, her nightmares.

"Go!" she orders. Clarice darts across the room and scales the shelves. They're thin, and if she hadn't seen someone else scale them before, she might not have believed how deceptively strong they were.

It takes her only a moment to reach the top. With the side of her head pressed against the ceiling, she leans over the top shelf as much and pushes aside stacks of papers until she sees a small air duct. The vent that covers it is barely bigger than her hand, and no air is flowing from it. As quickly as she can, she pulls the cover off and sets it to the side.

Clarice reaches into the duct and feels around. It doesn't take long for her to find what she's looking for. The tips of her fingers brush against a small handle, and she immediately grabs it. She then lowers herself to the ground with an old knife in hand before wiping away her tears.

Clarice inspects the weapon. The blade is less than three inches, and the steel it's made from is worn and pitted. The brass hilt is dusty, and the staghorn handle offers a good grip.

She turns the knife over and becomes drawn in by the reflection of light on the blade. She stares at it for God knows how long, and the only thing that brings her out of her self-induced hypnotic trance is the glimpse of movement out of the corner of her eye.

Clarice snaps her head up in time to see a male, tall, muscular, and with a strong jaw and strong hands enter the room. He's dressed in slacks and a long-sleeved polo that are torn and stained several times over. His brown leather shoes are cracked, and the soles are starting to split.

"Nick?" she says, backing up.

"It's okay, sweetie," he says, stepping toward her with one hand up. "I won't let them get you."

His dark eyes are filled with compassion, but Clarice knows that look. She knows the lie. "Please, don't," she whimpers.

Nick shakes his head. "I'm sorry. I'm so sorry."

In an instant he's upon her, and the two crash to the ground. Clarice fights for all she's worth. She struggles, punches, kicks, and bites, but she can't get out from under him. With a good sixty pounds of extra muscle on his side, Clarice hasn't a chance.

"It'll be over soon," he says, straddling her waist and wrestling the knife from her hand.

Clarice manages to get her hands on his wrist and stops the knife the moment he tries to cut her with it. But her stay on the attack is only temporary. Nick leans forward, putting all of his weight behind the handle, and the blade inches closer to her face with every passing breath.

"Stop!" she screams. In one last bit of defiance, she kicks the shelves next to her.

One of the shelves drops, and box after box of paper comes sliding off.

Clarice throws her hands up in front of her face and screams again. She thrashes about, taking hit after hit of heavy box. When it's over, she curls in a fetal position and whimpers softly.

Eventually, she peeks over her arm. The knife lies a few feet away, partially buried. For minutes, Clarice remains motionless, her eye fixated on the handle of the blade.

"Just memories, Clarice," she tells herself. "He's gone now. You know he is. Take the knife, Clarice. Take it and run before they find you."

A few more minutes pass before Clarice obeys. Stiffly, she pushes herself up and notices her already aching arms have started to bruise. But Clarice doesn't let such minor injuries delay her. She scoops up the knife, stuffs it into one of her pockets, and heads out the door.

When she gets back to the mailroom, the clerks are fighting over the last remnants of her offering. They bite and claw at each other as much as the papers in their hands, and not one takes notice of Clarice, nor her quick exit.

It's best they don't, she tells herself. For when they no longer have documents to devour, there's no telling what else they might feast on. Stories have always run rampant through the office about the black hole that is interoffice mail. Much goes in, and almost nothing comes out.

As she heads back to Toby, she wonders what he'll do once the cutting starts. She wonders if she can make him understand.

He'll have to, really. He has no choice.

CHAPTER SEVEN

It's a sunny morning at the zoo, and an open condiment packet sails through the air. Ketchup trails behind, promising to stain anything it touches without prejudice. The packet arcs into the tiger pit and splatters the ground near the zookeeper. Red globs hit his shoe, but he doesn't notice. No doubt he's more concerned with the three Bengal tigers nearby than he is about random encounters with flying tomato paste.

Eight-year-old Katie, on the other hand, with her nose cresting over the railing above, watches intently. A moment passes, and disappointment crosses the young girl's freckled face. She lowers herself to the sidewalk and stuffs her hands into the pockets of her bright blue windbreaker. She spends a moment rummaging around them before pulling forth a second pack of ketchup. Grinning, Katie bites a corner off, thereby arming yet another condiment grenade.

Toby watches the spectacle for a few moments, unsure why everything has a surreal nature to it or how he even got here, but he doesn't dwell such things long. He realizes he needs to play parent. "Give me that," Toby says, snatching it from her. "Are you trying to get us thrown out?"

Katie glares at her father with her green eyes. Though he's easily two feet taller that she is, she's unfazed by his scolding. "No, Daddy," she says, turning back to the tiger pit. She pulls herself up on the railing so her head crests over once again. "I'm trying to make the man more tasty."

"More tasty?" Toby echoes, unsure if he had heard correctly or whether or not he wants her to explain if he had.

"Yes, Daddy," she replies. She then points her finger at the sunbathing felines below. "I'm hoping they'll eat him if I do."

"Katie!" says Toby, tussling her brown hair. "Don't be like that."

"Like what?" she says, pulling back. "They should eat everyone here."

Toby raises an eyebrow. Clearly, his carnage loving princess hadn't thought her wishes through. "You want them to eat us as well?"

Katie lets go of the metal railing and drops down from her tip toes. "Yes," she says, but after a moment's thought, she amends her statement. "Well, maybe only bite you, Daddy."

"That's not very nice," Toby says, forcing a chuckle and extending an open hand to his little princess. "Why would you want something like that to happen? We're their friends."

Katie narrows her eyes, closes her lips tight, and plants her hands on her hips. "Daddy," she says. "We're not animal friends."

Toby reaches down, takes her by the wrist, and leads her down the red brick path. "Of course we are," he says. "You say it all the time."

"It's not nice to lock them up."

"It's dangerous in the wild, sweetie," Toby says, hoping it will placate her. "There's not a lot of tigers left in the world. We need to keep some in a zoo so we can always enjoy them. And that's a good thing."

"The only thing a zoo is good for is stripping an animal of its natural life for our selfish desires."

Toby stops in his tracks and stares at the diminutive stranger at his side. "Where on Earth did you hear that?"

"Mr. Tundley says it all the time," Katie replies. "He says locking animals up is mean, and anyone that comes to the zoo is just as bad as those that lock them up."

"Mr. Tundley is wrong," says Toby who is now annoyed at the third-grade teacher. "I promise the tigers like it here. All the animals do."

"Like how you said Collin liked it when I locked him in the tool shed overnight?"

"No," Toby says. His little girl's ability to argue dazzles him, and thoughts of her future in law school flash by. "It's not like that at all. Your little brother was scared and could have been hurt. The animals here are safe. They get free food and water, and don't have to worry about getting sick or injured. It's much better for them, I promise. And even if it's a little smaller than what they're used to, I'm sure they're still happy."

"They are not!" she says, small fists clenched at her side. "They want to run free and be with their family!"

Toby sighs and decides perhaps a new exhibit will be a good distraction. "Why don't we go see the marsupials?" he offers. "You like kangaroos. They have possums too. Maybe we'll see them play dead."

"Play dead?"

"Yes, it's what they do to trick predators."

"I know, Daddy," she says. "Did you ever think maybe they want to die? Maybe they'd rather be dead than be in your smelly zoo?"

"I promise they're fine," says Toby, wary of his little princess's growing anger. The redness in her face and the biting of her lip are telltale signs she's about to pop. "You really think people want to hurt them? Now come on, let's go find Mommy."

Katie pulls her hand away and stomps down the path, her leather boots clomping loudly as she goes. "You're a mean daddy!"

Toby shakes his head and starts after her. A chilly wind blows from behind and causes goose bumps to raise on his arms. Maybe the zoo wasn't the best idea after all. Maybe, he adds, he should have brought a jacket as well instead of just wearing the short sleeved polo shirt he had put on. A few paces into his chase, something stings the back of his neck. His vision wobbles and fades. At some point, Toby realizes he's fallen over, and he can taste blood in his mouth.

Toby tries to get to his feet, but the best he can manage is to roll over onto his back. People hover over him, silhouettes against a white, blown-out sky. Their words are muted in his ears. The last thing he's aware of are small hands patting his face and the sound of his daughter crying nearby.

Toby jolts awake.

A dark, feminine form slips under the covers next to him, and the mattress shifts. Her body warms his, and he slides a hand across her waist, drawing her close. "Am I glad to see you," he says. With his eyes still closed, he nuzzles into her neck and sighs. "Talk about some messed up dreams."

"Bad ones?"

"You have no idea."

"I'm sorry, Toby." Her body shifts and her voice is barely audible. "I'm so sorry."

For a half second, Toby wonders why his bride sounds so despondent. But then he realizes two things. One, it's not his bride, Nikki, that's talking to him, and two, her apology wasn't directed at his dream state.

His eyes open wide. Clarice looms over him, and he catches the glint of a small knife in her right hand.

"What the hell?" he spits out, but it doesn't stop the knife.

It dives through the air like a raptor after prey. Toby rolls off the bed, and the blade impales his pillow an instant later. As he hits the floor and comes to his feet, the side of his face feels warm and wet.

Toby leaps to the side and not a second too soon. The knife point sticks into the wall where his head was moments ago. Before Clarice can free the weapon, Toby charges and rams her with his shoulder. Clarice loses her grip on the weapon and smashes into the wall. As she slides to the floor, dazed, Toby grabs her by the neck. "You think you're going to kill me?"

"No," Clarice says, shaking her head and holding up a feeble hand to stop his assault.

Toby growls. There's no mercy for one who sought to take his life, sought to make his bride a widow and his princess and son fatherless. He leans into her, pinning her against the wall and readies a fist for the coup de grâce. As he does, her tear-filled eyes meet his and she whispers, "I don't want to die."

Toby freezes. He can't bring himself to kill someone so helpless, foe or not. Disgusted, Toby throws her to the ground. "Come near me again and I'll break your goddamn neck."

"It's not what you think," she says between coughs and choked sobs.

Toby ignores her and bolts out of the apartment in only his boxers. He stops, however, the moment he steps into the hall. At least a half-dozen vending machines line the walls on either side, and even though he was puking his guts out when he first came by, he's certain that the two water coolers at either end of the hall are new additions as well.

"Toby! Wait!"

The call from whence he came spurs Toby forward. He runs down the hall and hammers the elevator button.

Seconds tick by, and the elevator never arrives. Frustrated, impatient, and not wanting Clarice to make a sudden appearance, Toby runs into the nearby stairwell. He races downward, taking two—sometimes one leap—to reach landing after landing. His first instinct is to head to the ground floor where the lobby doors lead to the outside, but then he realizes nothing's changed. The doors will no doubt still be locked and streaking through the lobby in his boxers will certainly draw more attention his way. He needs a place to think.

Without any other ideas, Toby leaves the stairs once he hits the fourth-floor landing. He slows his sprint to a trot and stops when he sees the plethora of vending machines that line these walls as well.

Twenty yards away, one of Mr. Squid's relatives lugs a full duffle bag down the hall. He stops, whips out a plate-shaped device, and presses its center with the tip of a tentacle. A three-foot section of the wall disappears and reveals a tiny alcove. In the cubbie sits a bar stool, a flat-screen TV, and something that looks like a prop ray-gun from a 50s flick seen on Mystery Science Theater 3000.

The alien turns, notices Toby, and waves a friendly tentacle his way. Toby backtracks, not wanting to be anywhere near the space squid, and runs down the hall. After a few corners, he reaches the entrance to his office space. Toby plows through the double doors to the cubicle farm, and his flight grinds to a halt. Only the scantest of light illuminates the cubbies, making navigation difficult.

"Anyone here?" Toby calls out, despite the obvious lack of office life.

No one replies.

Toby fumbles in the dark and gropes the wall, but for the life of his shins and toes, he can't find a light switch. Several bruises and curses later, Toby manages to find a full-length window. He prays it happens to be his own. A feel to the right yields a door, and a turn of its knob lets him in.

"Oh, thank God," Toby says after finding and flicking the wall switch to his office.

Toby slams the door shut and pushes the button embedded in the handle. A test of the knob shows that it's locked, but the door isn't as secure as he'd like. The entire mechanism feels flimsy, and after peeking through his office window to check for nearby psychotic secretaries, he darts back into the farm and brings back the first chair he can find in the darkness. Once he's safe in his office, he wedges the chair under the door handle and collapses on the floor.

Toby stares at the carpet. His vision blurs. His body wants nothing more than to rest for a week, aftereffects of all the drugs and adrenaline he's sure. But his mind demands he stay awake, stay safe, and find a way home. "Think, think, think," Toby says, massaging his temples. "There has to be a way out. There has to be."

A series of taps on glass, light and fast, draw his attention. Clarice stands outside, pressed against the window. Her watery eyes lock on to Toby long enough to convey an unspoken plea before they dart left and right, scrutinizing the darkness surrounding their meeting.

Toby leaps to his feet. "Get away!"

Clarice jumps back. Her hands come up, and she crouches low. "Please, Toby," she says, her voice barely audible through the glass. "Let me in."

"I said get away!" Toby yells again. This time, however, he lunges forward and strikes the window with both palms.

The glass bounces with a thud.

Clarice crouches even lower, all but cowering now. Her hands shake like a heroin addict that missed her morning fix. "No, Toby," she pleads. "You don't understand. I'm not—"

"Leave!" He hits the glass again, harder than before. "I don't want anything to do with you, your escape, your—"

"Okay, okay," she interrupts. "I'm going. Stop yelling."

Toby nods, breaths deep, and keeps a wary eye on her.

Clarice reaches down and does something near the door he can't quite see. She then wipes her eyes and looks at him one last time before disappearing into the darkness.

Toby spends another hour staring out the window, waiting for her to return. When she doesn't, he creeps his way to his desk and sinks down into his leather chair. He's not sure what he's going to do, what he can do. But as he sits there and contemplates, there's one thing he's certain he will never do: sleep.

CHAPTER EIGHT

Clarice huddles in a ball on the stairs between the fourth and fifth floor, sobbing quietly. She tried to save Toby. She tried to warn him. But it's too late now. Maybe he'll be okay. Maybe. But for now, she knows, she's on her own.

One of the doors above opens and she chokes off her tears. To her relief, the footsteps go up, not down, and then another door opens and she's alone in the stairwell again.

"Need to get back to our room, Clarice," she says, her voice shaking as uncontrollably as her hands are. "Need to get back. Must get back before they come and find us here."

She grips the sides of her head and digs her nails into her scalp. "No, no, can't do that," she says. "Too many patrons this time. Not enough employees. They'll still come for you. They'll come to take you away. Think. Think. Think. Think."

She looks down at her abdomen and wishes she had the bump. "Must be special," she whispers, rubbing her tummy. "Have to be. Have to look like it. Make them believe."

Then an idea hits her. It's not perfect, and she doesn't know if she can pull it off, but she's beyond desperate.

Clarice jumps up and races to the sixth floor. Once she reaches the exit door, she steadies herself.

"Hello," she says, practicing the lines she's about to give. "I think we're pregnant. Can I have a test?"

It sounds good. She's still a little shaky, but hopefully she can pass it off as excitement due to pregnancy. She tries her line a few more times, and each one feels stronger than the last.

"We're ready," she tells herself. With that, she opens the door and boldly strolls forward.

The sixth floor is much like the fourth and fifth, as it has a long, blue hall with grey carpet that forms a circle with doors leading to various offices on both sides. These offices, however, aren't for workers. They're for the aliens who work here, and for the most part, humans aren't allowed here except for specific reasons. Everyone knows this. It's part of the new employee briefing.

The only place humans can go here on their own is either the infirmary or the maternity ward. The latter is precisely where she's headed.

She passes by a few aliens as she makes her way, all of which look like Freddie's little brother or sister. One of them even looks like Freddie himself, and she stiffens at the sight of him. But it doesn't take long for her to realize that he's not the CEO of Preser Tech. He's missing a few digits off his tail hand. To her relief, they all ignore her for the most part. Only one stops her and asks where she's going, to which she promptly replies, "Maternity."

She enters the waiting area to the maternity ward and quietly sits down on one of the black plastic chairs. The room she's in is small with harsh, white light and shiny white walls which cause her to squint no matter which direction she looks.

She's not sure what the rationale is behind such a lighting choice, but she suspects it has something to with the four corner-mounted cameras in the room. They want to see everything that happens here, and they want to see it well.

Across the room is a glass window, some two inches thick. On the other side sits one of the resident alien nurses, for a lack of a better description, who is currently examining a vial of something held in one tentacle. After a few moments, the alien places the vial on a small rack, turns its six bug eyes toward Clarice, and slides the window open.

"Hello dearie," it says, talking out of its elongated, tube-like mouth. "Think today is finally the day?"

Clarice stands, smiles, and walks over as calmly as she can. "I hope so."

"Well," the alien says, reaching into a nearby drawer and pulling out a plastic cup with a lid on it. "You know what to do. Would you like some water?"

"Water is good," says Clarice. "Thank you. Thank you very much."

The nurse reaches down and pulls out a Styrofoam cup before handing them both to Clarice. She then pushes a button and one of two doors next to the window beeps and opens, revealing a small bathroom inside.

Clarice enters without word. She fills her Styrofoam cup from the sink inside and drinks. The water has a slight metallic taste to it, but it's cool and refreshing. When she's done with that cup of water, she takes another, and a third, all the while shutting her eyes and trying quell her racing thoughts. She's got to get this right.

"You okay in there?" the alien calls out.

"I'm okay," Clarice replies. "I'm okay."

She drops her pants and sits on the toilet. The door remains open, which isn't a surprise. One of the cameras in the other room has a direct shot at her, and she knows the alien nurse is watching, waiting for her to pee.

But she doesn't. She sits for a few more minutes, ignoring any and all urges to go. When she feels that she's waited enough, Clarice gets up, pulls up her pants and goes to the window.

"Can't seem to go," she says. "Maybe if I walk a bit. Do some laps."

The alien shoos her toward the door. "Go on, dearie. Whatever you think will help."

Clarice goes for the door but is stopped when the nurse calls out once more. "Dearie," she says. "You need to leave your cup here, sweetie."

Clarice curses under her breath and reluctantly hands the plastic cup back. "Sorry," she says. "Forgot. Just excited, I guess."

"Course you are, dearie," the nurse says. "Come back when you're ready to go."

The window slides close and Clarice heads for the stairs. Though she's down one cup, she still has another, the Styrofoam one. Maybe her plan will still work. It has to. Clarice heads up to the tenth floor, the apartment section of upper management and higher ups. Getting some urine from Lexi, Preser Tech's newest mother-to-be, shouldn't be any harder in a Styrofoam cup than a plastic one. The hard part Clarice knows, aside from talking Lexi into such a thing, is going to be getting the pee from one cup into the other without being caught.

Clarice leaves the stairs and trots down the tenth floor hall. Everything about this place screams prestige. Golden wallpaper with a floral design hangs on the walls while rich, thick carpet sits on the floor, barely a week old and free of stain and scratch. The doors are heavy oak with silver knockers, and even the air smells crisp and spring-like.

Clarice picks up the pace, afraid she might be get caught. She thinks she remembers Lexi's room number from the directory, and when she gets to room 1020, she hesitates at the knocker. Even if this one is right, Lexi will likely flip out over such a late-night awakening

"Have to get a pink tag," she whispers. "Have to. Must. Have to try this one."

No one answers, and Clarice knocks again, louder and longer this time. A moment later, she hears the muffled sounds of someone cursing from inside the apartment. Clarice bites down on one of her knuckles and waits.

The door cracks open. Lexi peeks out, wrapped head to toe in a black comforter. She stares at Clarice with bloodshot eyes and says, "This better be important."

"Is important," Clarice replies. "Very, in fact. Have to talk to you about something."

Lexi scratches her head and clears her eyes. A lock of brown hair falls in front of her face which she lazily brushes away. "I'm sorry, who are you again?"

"Clarice," she replies. "Clarice. Freddie sent me," she lies. "Was concerned about something. Wanted to make sure you were okay. That the baby was. Sent me, he did. Freddie, I mean. Can I come in?"

"I can't believe this can't wait until morning," she says, this time more irritated than tired. "I'm a board member. I don't have to put up with this. Especially from someone like you."

Lexi tries to shut the door and Clarice jams her foot inside to keep it from closing all of the way. For a split second, the both of them look at each other with shock.

"Sorry, but I—" Clarice starts, but the board member quickly cuts her off.

Lexi's eyes narrow. "I'm calling H.R."

Clarice feels the color drain from her face. "No, please."

"Too late." Lexi spins around and goes back to her bedroom.

Operating on equal parts instinct and desperation, Clarice barges in the room and sees Lexi about to pick up her phone. Unlike the ones everyone else gets, the ones for board members work, and work well, and Clarice realizes she has more fingers on her hand than seconds to spare.

"What the hell are you doing in here?" Lexi shouts as she reaches for the receiver.

Clarice closes the distance between them in a flash and drives a fist into Lexi's nose. It crunches immediately, causing Lexi to shriek. Clarice then grabs the phone off the nightstand and whacks the woman across the top of the head.

The shrieking stops, and Lexi slumps to the ground. Clarice immediately kneels at the woman's side. She presses two fingers into her neck and finds a pulse. It's strong, and given that the board member is already stirring, she knows the woman will live and come to soon.

Clarice reaches for the pink tag on Lexi's ear, but decides against it. As much as she needs it, so does Lexi. Clarice considers leaving without it, but then realizes—prays is more like it—that the nurse at Preser Tech might have given Lexi a spare. After all, in all the time Clarice has been here, she has seen women wearing more than one on occasion.

Clarice ransacks the apartment in record time. She tosses clothes, drawers, and the mattress while Lexi slowly regains consciousness. After thoroughly tossing the bedroom, Clarice darts into the bathroom and tosses it as well, but to her dismay, no tag is to be found.

A groan comes from the bedroom, and Clarice knows she's out of time. She heads back to Lexi in order to strip her of her tag but stops when she sees how helpless the woman looks.

Unwilling to strip the woman of her only protection, all Clarice can do is hit the wall with her fist before running out of the door.

She'll find another way, Clarice tells herself. She'll have to. And in the meantime, hopefully, Lexi won't remember who to file a complaint against.

Hours pass before the lights flick on over the farm. The fluorescent bulbs hum to life and bathe the cubicles in a harsh, sterile light. People slowly file into the office, meandering about, snacking on doughnuts, sipping coffee, and making idle chatter. To Toby's delirious delight, Clarice isn't anywhere to be seen.

But Matt is. Toby catches sight of him right as the surfer rounds a corner and slams into Toby's office door.

"Dude!" he says, wearing the biggest grin Toby's ever seen. "Open up!"

Toby doesn't move, not because he's scared, but because he's exhausted.

"Come on, bro!" Matt says, pounding the door and trying the handle a few times. "Don't hang me out to dry!"

Toby capitulates with a sigh. He trudges over, moves the chair out of the way, and unlocks the door.

"Look at you, Mr. Big Kahuna!" Matt says, barging in and smacking Toby on the back. "You nailed her! I can't believe you charged right up on Clarice like that."

Toby blinks. "What?"

"You must have some wicked carves to nail your secretary your first day here, brah," says Matt. He adjusts his tie and flicks a piece of lint from his white dress shirt. "You gotta tell me your secret."

"I didn't do anything with her. I swear."

"Don't try and psyche me out, boxer dude," Matt says with a snicker and a point.

"Dude—" Toby says. He stops himself from continuing when it dawns on him that he's mimicking Matt to a tee. He then takes a deep breath and says, "I didn't have sex with her."

"It's nollie, I promise," Matt says. "And Freddie keeps saying you're his newest buck. Guess he was right on that!"

"I didn't—"

"Whatever, brah," Matt says. Annoyance crosses his face, and he folds his arms over his chest.

Toby lets the matter drop. "What now?"

Matt's eyes light up. "Dude! The season's starting!"

"What season?"

"Don't be a nutter," says Matt. "<u>The</u> season. And dude! You've got to get dressed for it. You can't be running around here in your boxers when they come. Freddie'll shut you down."

"I don't have anything to wear," Toby replies. "My clothes are gone."

Matt drums his fingers on his chest for a few beats. "Got it! I know right where you can get some."

"Let me guess, the mall?"

"Naw, there's a pile of clothes right outside your door."

Toby glances out the window. Sure enough, there's a light-brown pair of pants and matching short-sleeved shirt neatly folded next to the door. Toby stares at them, and given all of the weird crap he's been through as of late, he half expects the clothes to jump up and run off on their own.

"You better put them on, brah," Matt says. "We can hit the mall later."

Toby nods and complies. Surprisingly, the pants are a good fit. The shirt, however, is slightly baggy. "Not bad," Toby says, patting himself down. "Not bad at all." Toby looks up in time to see Matt smirk. "What?"

Matt shakes his head. "It says you're the janitor."

Toby looks down and sure enough, over his left breast pocket is an embroidered tag that reads, "Janitor."

"We've got to get you some new threads," Matt says with disdain. "I can't be seen hanging with the guy that cleans the crapper. If we hurry, we can get something before Freddie sees you and freaks the fuck out."

The elevator dings at the eighth floor, and the doors slide open. Matt takes the lead and steps off quickly. Toby is right behind, looking for an exit, but stops after a few steps. On the wall is a six-by-four-foot canvas with the picture of a man in a business suit, seated on the floor with Freddie standing proudly behind. The man is clutching a pen and legal pad, while Freddie himself has some sort of walking stick in hand. The background behind the two is severely out of focus, but Toby is pretty sure it's the cubicle farm, nonetheless.

"Last year, I think," Matt says. "That was...uh...Daniel something. He was the...um..."

"The VP of Communications and Investment Opportunities for the Acquisition of Hostile Companies," Toby finishes, reading the name badge. The willies crawl up his back, make a home on his neck, and throw a party.

"Wonder what happened to him," Matt remarks offhandedly. "Long gone before I got here."

Toby continues to stare at the picture but doesn't reply.

"His loss, brah," Matt says. "Let's get you set."

Toby snaps out of his trance, and Matt is a good ten yards ahead of him down the hall. As Toby breaks into a trot to catch up, Matt suddenly halts. The surfer's brow crinkles, and he takes several whiffs from the air with his nose.

"What?" Toby asks.

"Hang for a sec." Matt says, holding up a finger. He slowly moves through the hall until he comes to a closed, plain door and stops. "It's coming from in here."

"What is?"

"That smell," replies Matt as he opens the door. A red light, straight from a hooker's district, shines from inside and bathes his entire body. Matt's eyes go wide, and he starts to laugh.

Toby comes to the side of the door as Matt enters. A musky scent wafts from the room, and Toby's nerves are soothed. Both the floor and walls are bare, and there's not a single object save for a waist-high table and a body.

Matt hurries to the table, laughing all the way.

"What is it?" asks Toby, praying they haven't found a corpse.

"Dude, come here," Matt says with a wave. "Check this out."

Toby approaches with trepidation, but once he rounds Matt, the tension in his muscles vanishes, and he can't help but smile and shake his head in disbelief. On the center of the table, spread eagle, is a blow-up doll. Her vinyl arms are outstretched in a welcoming embrace. Her legs are wide and inviting. Her mouth is formed in a perfect "O", and her lips are full, red, and expecting. As Toby stares at her and the musky scent in the air grows stronger, he feels the urge to rub one out in the bathroom.

"Wanna tag team her?" Matt asks, unfastening his belt. "You can even pick which end you want."

"I'm not screwing a blow-up doll," says Toby. His words are hollow at this point since he's pretty sure he's about to give it a go.

"Might be the only tail you get for a while," Matt remarks. His pants and boxers hit the floor.

Toby ignores the fact that Matt now has an erection in hand. "What do you mean?"

"No one around here is going to fuck the janitor," he says. "At least, no one better than Suzy here," he adds, slapping her on the ass.

Matt flips Suzy over so her legs dangle to the ground and her arms prop her up on the table top. A second later, he's got her mounted and is working himself into a steady, humping rhythm. He slows to angle Suzy's head toward Toby's crotch. "She wants you, brah."

Toby can't deny it, nor does he want to. He can't stop gazing into her painted eyes. He reaches out and strokes her hair. Her vinyl skin, smooth and supple, bends to his touch.

"Oh yeah," Matt grunts. His face turns red. His jaw clenches, and his hands impose a death grip on Suzy's narrow waist.

Something explodes. A wet spray hits Toby's cheek, and he jumps back. Matt's eyes roll back in his head while a stupid, happy smile remains fixed on his face. A red blot appears on his chest, spreading and staining every fiber of his white dress shirt.

"Matt?"

Matt doesn't answer. He falls forward on Suzy. She holds him for a moment, then pops. Matt crashes to the ground. Blood pools around his chest while some leaks from his nose and mouth.

Horrified, Toby retreats two steps. "Matt? Matt?" he says, half expecting his words to miraculously heal his friend. "Get up, man. This isn't funny."

Toby catches a shimmer of light in the corner of his eye, and he turns to see two Freddie-like aliens slither out of a cubby in the wall—a cubby that Toby is certain was not there before.

The two aliens approach, chirping and chortling. The smaller of the two offers some direction to its companion, all the while holding a nondescript cube. Tall Freddie, so recently and aptly named, crouches next to Matt's body, and using his rearward tentacle, hoists Matt up by the head so the two are more or less the same height. Tall Freddie then adjusts Matt's name badge so it's plainly visible and gives a thumbs up. There's a click, a flash, and Matt's body thumps to the floor.

"Oh god," Toby says, wishing he could turn invisible. "Oh god. Oh god. Oh god."

Freddie was right. This isn't a zoo. It's a preserve. But it's not for conservation; this one's for hunting.

CHAPTER NINE

Toby eyes the exit. It's only twenty feet away, but the pair of Freddies are in the way, and he's worried that if he bolts for the door, they'll think he's charging them. And if they think he's charging them, he's pretty sure he'll be blown away. Then again, if he sticks around they might shoot him anyway.

Toby edges around the room and hopes his slow movements won't distract the aliens from their kill. Small Freddie continues to chirp, all the while constantly playing with and adjusting Matt's name badge. Tall Freddie, on the other hand, stands and looks down on the kill with an air of satisfaction. A few more seconds pass, and Toby has managed to creep nearly halfway around them both. Then Small Freddie looks up and makes eye contact.

Toby freezes. Before his brain can decide whether or not that was a good idea, Small Freddie speaks. "Go on, little jannie," it says with a shooing of hands. "Go get big and strong, and earn lots of promotions."

The alien whips out a device about the size of a deck of cards, and a rectangular portal appears in the room. It's nearly seven feet tall, two dimensional, and gives off a cool, blue glow.

Toby's thoughts escape his lips. "Holy shit."

Tall Freddie grabs Matt by the arms and drags him through the portal, disappearing completely. Small Freddie makes a beeline to the wall cubby they were in, scoops up a few things, and disappears through the portal as well. The portal flickers before vanishing, leaving Toby alone.

"Holy, holy, shit," he says, running his fingers through his hair.

Toby darts out of the room and spins around in the hall, unsure where to go. "I've got to get out of here," he says, thinking out loud. His mind wanders to Clarice, to Boris, to Melissa, to all the nameless others in the office that are about to have a bad, bad day. "I've got to warn them," he says to himself as he runs down the hall. A smirk crosses his face, and he shakes his head. "I've got to stop talking to myself, too."

The elevator, once again, proves too slow, and Toby launches himself down the stairs. He reaches the fourth floor and flies down the hall, hoping, praying that he doesn't become the next kill. Thankfully, he reaches the double doors to the cubicle farm without incident and bursts through.

Toby halts. The farm is empty, and the smell of fresh morning coffee hangs in the air. A breeze from a nearby floor fan blows past him, and for the moment, the fan's motor is the only thing he can hear. Toby holds his breath, and his prayer for sign of life is quickly answered. Muted laughter pours over the cubicles from the other side of the office. With a sharp sigh of relief, Toby investigates.

It takes only moments to find where everyone is. They are all in an elongated conference room, each seated around an extended, U-shaped desk while a sole presenter stands near a screen with a pie chart. The man is dressed in a suit fitted for someone three inches shorter than he, making his bare, wiry arms and legs even more pronounced than they would have been in proper attire. In his spidery hands, the man grips a keychain with a laser pointer attached and constantly makes a little red dot bounce around both his presentation and the room.

Toby goes for the door, but as soon as he does, one of the room's occupants takes notice of him through the window and beats him to the punch. The door cracks open and out pops the head of a rotund man with one of the worst comb-overs Toby has ever seen. The man motions to a small table to his left and says, "Get the wastepaper basket underneath, but leave the doughnuts and juice."

Toby does neither and pushes by, intent on addressing them all ASAP.

"What is the meaning of this?" the presenter says, a burning scowl upon his face. "This is a private meeting."

From the back of the room someone calls out, "Isn't that Clarice's new boss?"

"No way," someone else says.

"Actually, I think he might be," chimes in a third.

The presenter's face loses its crimson look and is replaced with a hint of dread. "Clarice?" he says, looking to the far corner of the room. "Now where the devil did she go?"

Toby looks to his right to where an empty chair is. He's not sure if that was indeed where Clarice sat, or what advantage having her here might be, but since he has nothing else to use at the moment, he decides to play the VP card in the hopes it will get people to listen. "She's running an errand for me," he says, interjecting as much authority as he can in his voice. "Do you have a problem with that?"

The presenter's face pales, and he fumbles over his words. "My apologies," he says. "The janitor uniform threw me off, sir."

Toby straightens and brushes off his shoulders. "Never mind the uniform," he says. "I need everyone's attention right now."

"Of course," the man says, bowing and scooting sideways. "I would always yield the floor to you, sir."

"Okay, everyone, listen up," he says, composing his thoughts so he can slip into the role. "What I'm about to say may scare you, but it's important you know what's going on. Matt is gone—"

A collective "eep" comes from the crowd.

"—yes, Matt is gone. I couldn't save him—"

"I'm sure it wasn't your fault," someone says.

"Thank you, but what I need everyone to understand is that unless we do something right now, we're all next."

"Oh God, we're getting fired," someone says.

"I can't lose my benefits!" says another.

A hand shoots up. "What about our retirement?"

Then another. "Is this because he never filled out his 624-VL forms in triplicate when requesting new reams of paper?"

Three more arms raise, then six, and before Toby can blink twice, the entire room is a sea of hands reaching for the ceiling, and a game of "who can shout the loudest" is in full swing.

Initially, it's too much for Toby to take in, and he stares, dumbfounded. Fortunately, it doesn't take long for him get in gear.

"Everyone be quiet," he says. But they don't stop. The questions come harder and faster. The cork on his bottle of self-control bursts and anger fountains out in the most magnificent of displays. He grabs a nearby, empty chair and slings it across the room. The impromptu missile nails the projector, and they both tumble to ground with an expensive-sounding crash.

"Shut the hell up and listen!" Toby bellows. "Christ, no one is getting fired, but you're going to die if you don't shut up and pay attention! Do you hear me? You. Are. Going. To. Die!"

The room goes deathly silent.

The projector lies broken in two on the floor. A spark pops from its cracked shell, and the machine turns off.

Toby looks down at his fists and forces them to unclench. His fingernails have dug mini canyons in the palms of his hands. A few seconds pass, and it dawns on him that he's breathing like a raging bull. He grits his teeth and forces himself to slow. He has to remain in control or else he's not organizing anything; he's not escaping anywhere. As he recomposes himself, a timid hand raises from the back row. "Yes?" says Toby.

"When you say, 'die,' do you mean we're getting our hair done again?"

"I bet that's why Matt got fired," someone else says. "Probably missed his appointment with the stylist yesterday."

Toby, stupefied, blinks. "Matt didn't get fired."

"Well, transferred."

"He's dead!" Toby shouts. "D-E-A-D, dead!"

Whispers float around the room, but the concern on the crowd doesn't seem to be with Matt's demise, but rather with Toby himself.

"They killed him!" Toby goes on. "He was shot. Killed. Blown away. Terminated."

"So he did get fired," says a petite blonde in the back. "I don't see why you had to break the projector though. Is this some sort of team building exercise?"

"Maybe the projector is a metaphor for Matt's job performance."

Toby throws up his hands in disgust. "You guys are hopeless," he says. "I'm getting the hell out of here. I suggest you all follow if you know what's good for you."

"We're moving the meeting?"

"But this is such a nice conference room."

"And we have doughnuts here!"

Toby groans. The urge to throw something else is nearly unmanageable, but there's nothing heavy enough in arm's length to satiate the desire. "No," he says, redirecting his energy. "I'm leaving this place. The building. The company. In short, I'm going home, with or without you."

Eyes go wide. Fear, panic, and disgust wash over the crowd of faces like a tsunami.

"Is he serious?"

"He can't leave us like that, can he?"

"What could possibly be better than the office?"

"I'm not feeling very happy!" The last line sparks something in a few people, and they make a mad dash for the doughnut and juice table and scarf down both drink and bakery delight with reckless abandon.

Toby goes for the door, but a staying hand from the presenter keeps him in the room. "Get off me," Toby orders, eyes narrowed.

"With all due respect," the presenter says. "Maybe you should have something to eat and relax. You're getting the troops nervous. It's bad for productivity."

Toby shrugs him off. "Screw productivity. Screw the troops. Screw the whole damn place."

There's a shriek in the room. "Someone make him a team player!"

Before Toby has even the inkling to figure out who shouted the remark, he's tackled from behind. He hits the ground face first, but he doesn't give in. He flips over like the master ninja he pretended to be when he was nine and strikes out. A hammer fist, his own, hits the inner thigh of a nearby office assistant, and the woman falls back, crying out in pain. A dingy, white-collared exec goes to stomp on his chest, but Toby beats him to the kick and drives the heel of his left foot into the man's groin.

"Bring it!" Toby yells, ignoring two blows to his ribs to issue two more attacks of his own.

The crowd answers the challenge with incompressible jeers and cries. They mass around him, punching, kicking, and grabbing. Soon his muscles tire, and in a momentary lull, a portly man in a patched-up grey business suit belly flops on Toby's chest. The air bursts from Toby's lungs, and a dozen hands pin him to the ground.

"Get off me!" Toby yells.

"Give him the juice!"

"A dozen doughnuts as well!"

A woman wails in the background. "Can't we just be happy and sing HR policies?"

Fingers clamp around Toby's neck. Stronger ones force his mouth open enough for a plastic funnel to be inserted. Toby tries to spit it out, and all he gets for his effort is a flood of orange juice in his mouth. He chokes it down and coughs. The fruity deluge doesn't stop. A seemingly endless stream of it comes through the funnel. And as Toby spits, splattering his face and shirt with both saliva and orange juice, he feels his will to fight fade. His muscles relax. A fog begins to settle over his mind, and he knows time is short. Memories of his bride, his princess, his son, are fading fast.

Toby spies a nearby ballpoint pen under the table. As he locks on to it with his eyes, he stops his protest and smiles. Seconds pass, and a warm, gooey feeling envelopes him. He bites down on the inside of his cheek, hard. Blood trickles into his mouth. Pain stabs through his head, but it's only enough to slow the drugs, not stop their ill effect. He lies there, still smiling, and bites the inside of the other cheek as well.

Hands tentatively ease their grip, then let go altogether.

Toby doesn't move at first. He stares at the ceiling and silently repeats Nikki's name over and over. He sits up quickly and brushes off his shoulders, still clinging to his bride's memory. "That was...embarrassing," he says.

"You okay, sir?" someone asks.

Toby gives a playful scowl. "Not when there's still work to be done." He scoops up the ballpoint pen before taking to his feet. The office crowd gives him room but still looks upon him with suspicion. "Don't suppose there's an éclair left, is there?" he asks, popping the pen into his mouth.

To his delight, the crowd collectively turns to the snack table. In that instant, Toby chomps down on the pen, splitting its plastic shell. He sucks on the broken ballpoint for all he's worth. Ink fills his mouth and coats his tongue and throat. It takes every fiber of his being to hold a poker face and to keep from expelling the contents of his stomach onto those around him. But at least the warm fuzzies fade. At least he can picture Nikki's bright smile once more, his children's playful laugh.

"There's an éclair right here!" someone cries out.

The pastry is quickly shuffled to Toby. He bites a piece off and hopes his Bic inoculation will last. "This is really good," he says, chewing slowly. He pushes by the few people that stand between him and the door. "Continue the meeting," he says. "I need a few reports from my office."

"Very good, sir," the presenter says.

The door closes behind Toby and the moment he is around the corner and out of sight, he spits out the masticated dessert. He grabs a handful of Bic pens from a nearby cup and breaks them open one at a time and sucks down their contents. Bile rises in his throat, and he chokes it down.

Out the double doors Toby goes, and he hurries as fast as he can without breaking into a full run. He rounds the last corner before the stairs and slows to a casual walk. At the far end of the hall, an office worker takes note of Toby. Thankfully, all the man does is wave before bending over and filling a plastic cup at one of the newly installed water coolers.

Toby smiles and sighs in relief. He continues to walk and rubs his temples in an effort to combat the insurmountable stress on his psyche. Something zips past his ear, and he looks up to see the coworker get impaled in the chest by a slender, black shaft that pins him to the cooler.

Toby screams, not out of fear or anger, but out of a sheer refusal to accept his fate. He charges down the hall, down the stairs, all the way to the first floor. As he runs through the lobby center, Melissa sits at her desk, smiling exactly how he'd left her the day before.

"Welcome to Preser Tech!" she says in her bubbly voice.

Toby skids to a stop as he comes to her side. "Up!"

He says it with such force that the receptionist obeys without hesitation. She stands there, bewildered, and Toby grabs her chair and charges the front doors with his makeshift battering ram.

His first strike is heavy. He can feel the power behind the blow in the shockwave that ripples through the chair and up his arms. The doors, however, don't budge. The glass doesn't chip, let alone break. Regardless, Toby remains undaunted. He brings the chair back and swings again and again. The glass wavers and thumps with each strike. By the time the muscles in his arms give out, all Toby's managed to do is knock off each and every one of the chair's wheels.

"Toby!" Melissa scolds. "You stop destroying company property this instant!"

Toby lowers the chair. "Look," he says, panting. "You can either stand there and look pretty and die, or you can help me escape."

"Why would I need to dye my hair if I already look pretty?"

Toby groans and rolls his eyes. "Not you, too," he mutters. "Screw it."

He raises the chair and slams it into the door one more time, splitting the chair's back in the process.

"Freddie is going to make you take a furniture-sensitivity class if you keep that up," Melissa says.

Toby goes to say something snide but stops when he spies movement off to the side. He squints, and there, in a tall, covered trash bin, he sees a hiding alien who's pointing something at Melissa.

Without a second thought, Toby rockets across the lobby floor, vaults over the reception desk, and tackles her at the shoulders. They hit the floor with a thump, and Melissa's coffee cup explodes, showering them both in a cold double latte.

"Oh, Toby," she giggles from underneath him. Her cheeks blush, and she rolls her eyes. "Like I'd ever have sex with a janitor."

Toby pushes off her and is about to try and pull her to safety when the large, meaty paw of Boris clamps down on his shoulder. "You try and steal Boris's girl again?"

Toby is spun around and catches a solid fist with the right hinge of his jaw. The force of the blow knocks him back around, and Toby collapses in a heap on the desk. His vision swims in a sea of colorful lights, and his ears take nothing in but a steady ringing. He's vaguely aware of being hoisted in the air before finding himself flying through the lobby.

Toby hits the ground and tumbles until he hits a wall. His vision clears fast enough to see a massive black boot driving down on him. Instinctively, Toby rolls out of the way, and Boris's foot stomps the ground where his face was a moment ago.

Toby scurries to his feet, but not before he catches a reinforced toe to the hip. "Stop being such a goddamn

Neanderthal," he says, with a wince. "I saved your girlfriend's life!"

Boris approaches, fists raised like a champion boxer. "You not talk your way out of this."

Toby brings his arms up as well and keeps moving lightly on his feet. He'd suspected it before, but now that he's actually been hit by the brute, he knows he'll never be able to go toe-to-toe and live. But staying in a fighting stance seems to have at least made Boris wary, and Toby hopes he might be able to keep him at bay long enough to escape before getting his skull crushed.

Boris's hesitation ends, and the guard lunges forward with a left jab. Toby jumps back, and Boris immediately follows with a right cross that grazes the side of Toby's head. Reflexively, Toby answers with a left jab of his own, and to his surprise, manages to connect with the guard's cheek.

Boris steps back, growls, and undoes his belt. Mace, gun, and keys thud on the floor. "You have fight in you," he says, cracking his knuckles. "I'll enjoy tearing arms from socket."

"Don't be such a dumbass," says Toby. "You're going to die if you don't knock this off."

Boris smirks. "You are big in talk, but small in deed."

Toby doesn't get a chance to reply before Boris hits him with a bull charge. The guard catches Toby around the waist and drives him backward. Toby rains elbow after elbow, punch after punch on top of the brute's head, but none have any effect. Toby impacts the wall with his spine, and he's certain at least two ribs crack in the process.

"Maybe next life you'll leave girl alone," says Boris. The fingers on his left hand close like a vice around Toby's neck, and he draws back his right in a tight fist. "Time to die."

Boris's eyes flicker. His body wobbles. He coughs once before his grip weakens, and his hand drops. Then, like a marionette whose puppeteer is having a heart attack, he slides to the floor with periodic spasms. A metal rod sticks out of his back, and from it, an all-too-familiar red pool forms.

Toby scurries to the side. Melissa is on her back, draped over her desk. Her hair and arms dangle to the ground. Her eyes look empty, and half of her face is caked in blood. Behind her, Mr. Squid ruffles through her clothes with his tentacles. Next to him, Mrs. Squid—for she's slimmer and dressed in pink—shoulders what has to be a spear gun and levels it right at Toby's chest.

"Oh damn," he says, inching sideways. He wonders how fast that thing will fly, or if he can even see it coming, let alone dodge it. All those wonderings immediately cease when he's tackled from the side.

Toby drops to the floor like a heap of bricks. There's a flurry of red hair in his face. Kisses assault his cheeks and lips. A tongue darts in his mouth, and hands grip his shoulders.

"Clarice!" he sputters out, too shocked to push her off. "What are you doing?"

Clarice, who is now straddling his waist, stops ravishing him long enough to glare and answer. "Quiet!" she orders. "Fuck me if you want to live."

Toby balks, unable to understand the rationale to her demand. Clarice, however, doesn't wait for him to react. She sheds her blouse and smothers him in kisses. As she does, she wedges a hand between them both, and pops open his shirt, sending buttons flying.

"Clarice—"

The secretary nibbles his ear and slides her hand into his pants. "Toby," she whispers. "I'm off limits—*you* are off limits—if we're mating. Now fuck me like I'm the last piece of ass you'll ever have because I just might be."

Toby nods and forces a smile. He glances at Mr. and Mrs. Freddie who are still in the lobby watching. Though Mrs. Freddie still has a spear gun in hand, she's lowered it for the moment. His view of them is short lasting, as Clarice turns his face to meet hers with a gentle hand on his cheek.

"Don't look," she says. "God, don't look."

With one hand, Toby reaches behind her and deftly pops open the clasp on her bra. Clarice pulls her hand from his pants long enough to let the garment slide from her shoulders and fall to the floor. Said hand then plunges back between them and goes for the button and zipper to his pants.

Toby shuts his eyes and tries to force the image of a pair of hunting, voyeuristic aliens from his mind. He runs both hands down her neck and chest, cupping her breasts before trailing his fingertips over her back. He leans up, kisses her shoulder, and works his way up to her mouth. Cold air brushes his groin, and a glance downward shows that Clarice has managed to get his pants down to his knees.

Despite the fact that her body is soft and warm and her curves near perfect, his performance is lacking, and he suspects that no pill on Earth would be able to help. After all, that damn smiling Bob never had to deal with this kind of pressure. Clarice, on the other hand, looks unfazed. She breathes heavily into his ear and wraps her fingers around his little man, a semi at best, and strokes it evenly. To Toby's relief and guilty pleasure, little Toby responds to her coaxing and turns into the tall, proud warrior he's known since puberty.

"Not bad," she whispers. She adjusts her grip on his erection, pulls him into her, and groans. "God, you feel good," she says, panting, rocking.

Toby's primal male takes over, and he flips her onto her back. His hands clasp hers, and each thrust of his pelvis builds a harder and faster rhythm. Clarice's moans grow loud enough to make even the most seasoned porn star blush. In the back of his mind, Toby understands it's all show, but he doesn't care. It's hot. *She* is hot, and the very Y side of his chromosomes is enjoying every last minute of it.

Toby turns his head at the sound of a nearby grunt. A dozen feet away, Mr. and Mrs. Squid have Boris's body hoisted between the two of them and are now awkwardly carrying him to a portal that's standing in the middle of the lobby.

"Harder, damn it," Clarice says, turning his face one more.

Toby complies, redoubling his effort. Heat builds between the two. Sweat pours from his forehead, runs down his back. Beads of water pool between her breasts, making the perfect target for his next kiss. But each and every moment he's screwing her brains out and feeling her nails dig into his back, he's watching the Squids.

They're about to enter the portal, Boris still being carried between the two, when a sudden influx of pressure builds in his groin. The tension works its way up his back and signals an impending grand finale. Toby bites his lip and closes his eyes.

Clarice locks her legs on his hips, grinding their sex fest to halt. "Get off me!"

Toby's eyes go wide with shock. His mouth hangs open, and an ill-formed, unintelligible question tries to pop out, but mostly it's the noise of a stuttering idiot.

"Get off! Get off!" she orders once more. Clarice squirms out from under him, apparently uncaring about the fact she has given Toby the worst case of blue balls he's had in a long time.

Toby watches her grab her blouse before finally managing to spit out, "What?"

Clarice points. "It's open! It's still open!"

Toby looks over his shoulder, back to where the Squids were, and sure enough, the portal is still open. Neither Mr. or

Mrs. Squid are about, but Melissa's body is still draped over the reception desk.

"Move!" Clarice says, pulling him up.

Hope springs up in Toby's soul, and the two make a dash for the portal. Toby's run is more of a hopping at first, for it takes a second to pull his pants up from his knees. But he manages to get them up with minimal stumble, and by the time he's got them zipped, Clarice has pulled him through the portal.

CHAPTER TEN

Toby takes in the scene. Goosebumps spread over his body. His breath hangs in the frosty air a good five or six seconds before disappearing. Angled, metallic walls—smooth, shiny, and an electric blue—shape the room into an egg. A vaulted ceiling stretches high overhead, and from it, dangle the upside down bodies of dozens of office coworkers. They gently sway in an artificial breeze generated by noisy, unseen fans. At the far end of the room, Mr. and Mrs. Squid hang Boris on invisible suspensions. Worse yet, there are at least another half-dozen aliens tending to their own kills as well. Thankfully, none of them are aware of Toby's and Clarice's arrival.

"Come on," she whispers, tugging his arm.

Toby obeys and keeps his eyes riveted on the aliens as she leads him out of the room and down a side passage. The hall, made of the same reflective blue material as the room before, winds a short way before ending at a large, grey door frame. Beyond it is simply a wall, as flat and hard as the others. Nearby is a narrow, marble pedestal on which sits a large, black disk.

Embedded in the disk are a number of much smaller disks arranged in concentric circles, each having a unique white glyph etched into its face. In the very center of the pedestal is a small cylinder that's no more than an inch wide and maybe twice that tall.

"What now?" asks Toby, glancing nervously over his shoulder.

Clarice points. "That pedestal has to open another portal or something."

"Why?"

"Because I'm not willing to consider anything else."

Toby lets a tiny laugh slip. "Okay. Any ideas on how to get it to work?"

"Nope. But it's all yours if you want."

"Well, here goes nothing," he says with a shrug. Without knowing what else to do, Toby pushes down on the cylinder. It sinks down a half inch before clicking into place. Immediately, the disks light up, some only slightly, but a few shine bright. The glyph of one disk, however, blinks steadily. Toby, hoping nothing will explode, sucks in a breath and presses the blinking glyph with his thumb. A low hum fills the air, and the blinking is replaced by a bright glow.

"Try another," says Clarice.

And so Toby does. He picks one at random and gives it a push. The hum in the air drops in pitch, and a portal, as cool and blue as all the others he's seen, fills the doorway.

Clarice exhales. "God, I hope this leads out."

"Me too," he says, feeling tension build in his neck and shoulders.

Clarice steps toward the portal, but Toby stays where he is. He doesn't like not knowing or seeing where he's about to go. Clarice, on the other hand, grabs his arm and pulls him through without hesitation.

Toby stumbles as he comes out the other side, but Clarice's iron grip keeps him upright. Dark brown, stony walls curve around them, and a domed, lighted ceiling sits on top. Before Toby can take in the details of where they are, the most horrid of screeches fills the air.

Startled, Toby jumps, breaking free of Clarice's grasp. He spins around the moment he touches down and sees a Mrs. Squid pointing at them with one of her tentacles. He hasn't a prayer to understand what she's saying in her rapid, alien language, but he figures it can't be anything good.

A circular door behind the alien opens, and in rush two Freddie look-a-likes, each fumbling to pull out their sci-fi sidearms that hang from their belts.

"Don't move," Clarice whispers, grabbing Toby by the arm. "Be dumb. Always be dumb."

Despite Clarice's warnings, Toby isn't convinced that's the best course of action. His brain furiously searches for an option that doesn't involve being led back to the slaughter house.

The two Freddies stop a few paces in front of Mrs. Squid, and the fatter of the two then slithers forward a couple of feet, blaster drawn but pointed downward. "Here persies," Fattie Freddie says, crouching slightly and extending its free hand. "Don't be scared."

Clarice stays rooted in place, but Toby takes a wary half-step back. As he does, he feels her tighten her grip on his arm.

"How did you little fellas get up here?" Fattie Freddie says, slithering forward a few more feet. "Let's get you back to The Farm where you belong."

Toby throws a glance to Clarice at The Farm's mention. While the alien could be speaking about Preser Tech, Toby suspects he is not. Clarice, however, seems just as clueless as he is about the reference and doesn't say a word.

"Come on," Fattie Freddie says. "Come on. It'll be okay."

Mrs. Squid begins to screech once more, but Fattie Freddie whips around and silences her with the raise of his hand.

"Don't mind her," Fattie Freddie says, turning back around. "She's just happy to see you. We only want to get you back to The Farm where it's safe."

Fattie Freddie eases forward and comes to a halt four feet from Toby and Clarice. Though his weapon is still drawn, the alien still has it pointed to the ground, and as best as Toby can tell, the alien isn't expecting an attack. And if he's not expecting an attack, Toby thinks, it might be possible to wrestle that gun away and use it to shoot their way out of this nightmare.

Clarice squeezes Toby's hand. "No, Toby," she says. "He's only trying to help. Trying to see us home."

Fattie Freddie puts an arm around Toby and directs him to a side hall. "Come boy," he says. "Let's get you back to your janitorial duties."

As Toby is pulled along, he turns around and tries to plant his feet. "What about her?" he says, looking straight at Clarice.

"Raegul will help her, don't worry, persie," says Fattie Freddie. "She'll be fine."

The moment Fattie Freddie finishes answering, Raegal, the other armed alien, slithers up to Clarice, takes her by the hand, and escorts her toward the one and only door in the room.

Tension builds in Toby's body, and time seems to slow. He knows must make a choice, right here, right now. He can go along and play dumb, and ultimately wind back up on the preserve dodging water coolers and blow up dolls, or he can take a stand here and now and fight for his life.

Toby glances at Fattie Freddie who in turn looks him over. Their eyes meet, and Toby smiles before giving Fattie Freddie a right cross.

Toby's fist hits Fattie Freddie square in the chin. The alien spins and crumples to the floor. Toby doesn't waste a moment seeing if the alien stays down. He charges toward Clarice and Raegul, his legs driving him forward with powerful strides. Mrs. Squid howls, and Raegul turns as Toby leaps through the air. Raegul tries to raise his gun, but the alien isn't fast enough. Toby drives his fist into the center of Raegal's face with a satisfying crunch.

Like his counterpart, Raegul drops to the floor. The alien's gun hits the ground, as does something else completely unexpected: a small, rectangular box. It's a portal device. No doubt about it. For a half second, Toby stares at them both, unable to believe his good fortune. A weapon and a key home delivered to his feet.

Toby dives for the gun, but Clarice knocks it across the room with a swift kick.

"What the hell did you that for?" Toby yells.

"They'll shoot you if you're a danger," she says.

"They're going to shoot us anyway!" Toby yells, shaking his head. Why this isn't painfully obvious to the woman, he'll never know. But now isn't the time nor the place to be having a long, thoughtful conversation on the matter.

Toby snatches the portal device, grabs Clarice by the arm and yanks her toward a nearby door. The other side reveals a long, stone hall. They run down it, passing several circular doors on the right as the hall slowly curves to the left. Toby doesn't dare slow because if Fattie Freddie and Raegul aren't back on their tails and in hot pursuit, the other aliens Mrs. Squid undoubtedly called are.

"Any idea where to go?" he asks.

"No," she says. "We need get out of these halls."

A small alcove appears as Toby and Clarice run on. Inside is a small, spiral ramp. Clarice skids to a stop, and pulls Toby's arm so he's forced to halt as well.

"Down here," she orders.

Toby balks. "Why?"

"Why not?"

Toby shrugs and the two take the ramp down ten, fifteen, twenty feet before being dumped out on a new floor. The walls are of the same dark, stony construction as before, but the doors set in them—doors with half windows and horizontal bar handles—remind Toby of the same ones that litter every public school he'd ever been in.

"Go in?" he asks, leaning on the bar.

Clarice nods, and Toby pushes the door open.

As they step through, they enter a wide-open hall with lockers lining the walls on both sides. Two-foot, square tiles decorate the floor and are arranged in a green and white checkerboard pattern. Their footsteps echo loudly upon it. The scent of heavy air freshener lingers, while harsh fluorescent bulbs illuminate the hall.

Clarice takes him by the hand and leads him forward. "No time to slow," she says. "No time at all. They'll be on us quick."

"Right," Toby says.

The two barely move a dozen paces before Clarice's prophecy comes true. Near the far end of the hall, three Freddies appear, sidearms drawn. Despite their alien nature, Toby can see both in their face and their posture they mean business.

The Freddie in the lead points directly at Toby and Clarice with his tail, and shouts, "Bad persies! You stop right there!"

Toby reflexively halts while a fourth Freddie and a Mr. Squid come through the doors that lead to the ramp, equally armed and looking non-to-pleased at having to chase free-roaming people.

Clarice clamps her hand on Toby's forearm. "Oh, god. Oh, god," she says over and over. "Said not to run. Said that was bad."

Toby pries her fingers off of him, and he takes her hands in his. Her body trembles, and all he can see in her eyes is an immeasurable amount of fear. How she's not running in a full state of panic is beyond him.

"Don't fall apart on me," Toby says, lifting her chin so she's looking right at him.

Clarice shakes her head, but doesn't reply.

Toby glances left and right. Both groups of aliens are methodically closing in. Each one looks ready for trouble, and Toby doubts he'll be able to sucker punch one again. Even if he could, there's no way he'll take on five aliens at once and come out on top.

"This is it," Clarice says, seeming to share a similar sentiment. "This is where it ends."

"No," Toby says. He narrows his eyes, looks past her to a single door with a round knob, exactly like the ones back home, just ten feet away. He's not about to let them take him away like lamb to the slaughter house.

With an explosive move, Toby surges toward the door, half dragging Clarice along. How she manages to stay on his feet, Toby doesn't know, but he gives a silent thanks to whoever may be watching over them that she remains upright. The two barrel through the door, and he's quick to slam it shut behind them.

"Welcome to Preser Tech!" says a chorus of voices in perfect unison.

Toby, with a death grip on the doorknob, spins around. Thirty or so girls, all in their early teens, all dressed like they raided their career-oriented mother's wardrobe, sit behind small, wooden desks in nice, neat rows. In front of them and at the head of the class stands an older woman near a chalkboard, mid-fifties, with a long, tattered and stained sundress, and cat-eye reading glasses. With one hand on her hip and another thoughtfully posing under her chin, she smiles and says to the class, "And what else?"

The class giggles and says together, "We're so glad to have you aboard!"

Toby jumps as something hits the door behind him. It takes all his strength to keep the handle from turning. A part of him wonders how long he can keep it closed, while another part wonders when they'll simply blast their way in. Hopefully, it won't come to that because they won't want to risk shooting the wrong person.

"Open up, persie!" comes a call from the outside hall. "We only want to make sure you're safe."

That call and a subsequent thump against the door spur Toby into action. With his free hand, he spins Clarice around. "Get me a chair!"

Clarice, visibly scared out of her mind, stares at him blankly. "What?"

"Get me a chair, damn it!"

Clarice shakes her head. "They're all bolted to the floor."

Toby scans the room and realizes she's right. That said, the teacher's chair looks free.

"Get that one," he says, pointing to it. "That should hold them for a bit."

Clarice sinks to the ground and curls into a little ball. "No, no, no," she says. "No barricade..."

"Damn it, Clarice," Toby yells. "Get me that chair and get it now!"

Clarice wraps her arms around her head and rocks. "They're coming, Nick," she says. "They're coming. God, do something!"

"Clarice! If you don't move now, we're dead!"

The secretary doesn't budge, and Toby, out of ideas, wonders how many of them he can take down before they get him.

CHAPTER ELEVEN

The handle turns, and Toby tightens his grip before cursing the world that has sucked Clarice into its shadowy depths. With seconds left to his life, Toby has an idea. He keeps one hand on the door knob while pressing his entire weight against the door and then reaches into his pocket and pulls out the portal device. It's silver and smooth, and try as he might, Toby can't find a single button, knob, or protrusion of any kind that would operate it.

Despite that setback, he randomly pushes all over its surface, hoping and praying something will happen. He even bangs it against the wall a few times. He's about to give up when glyphs appear on its skin.

"Hot damn!" he shouts.

The brief celebration draws Clarice back to the present. She stops rocking and looks up to Toby with hopeful eyes. "What?"

"I got it," he says, pressing glyphs at random with his thumb. He has no idea what he's doing, but then again, he didn't when he got the portal working in the freezer as well.

There's a crackling in the air and the smell of ozone hits Toby's nose. A portal springs out of the ground, tall, blue, and promising freedom. Clarice dives through with Toby following right on her heels.

The portal closes behind them, and now that Toby is on the other side, it takes his eyes a few seconds to adjust to the dim light. Once they do, he sees that they are in another hall, but instead of being cold and sterile, it's warm and cozy. Carved teak panels cover the walls, and mahogany boards line the floor with a finish so perfect he could use it to shave. Candelabras hang from the ceiling and bathe the area in a soft, yellow light. The smell of smoke drifts from some unknown place, and upon the very same air carries the sound of alien chatter, muted, but jovial.

"Feels like a lodge," whispers Clarice.

"No like about it," Toby replies. "I bet you're right on."

Clarice says no more, and for the first time in their bizarre relationship, Toby takes both her hand and the lead. "Aliens have to leave too," he says. "Let's find the exit."

Clarice follows, and though she's silent as they travel down the hall, her hand tightens on his and trembles.

"We'll make it out," he says.

"I know." Her hands shake a little more. "I know. I know. I know."

Toby squeezes her hand, hoping to alleviate her fears. "I mean it, Clarice. We didn't come this far to fail now."

Clarice relaxes. Doors pass by at regular intervals, heavy oak ones with wrought-iron handles. Toby doesn't take any of them. They each have a different glyph embedded on their center that reminds him too much of hotel rooms. The last thing he wants to do is barge in on an alien who's enjoying some R&R.

They round a corner, and an alien that looks like an undulating sack of potatoes with four arms and three legs enters the hall from a far off door. With three of its hands it keeps a book in its face and turns the pages. With its fourth, it closes the door behind it.

Toby immediately plows through the door to his left and yanks Clarice in. Relief washes over him, not only for the fact that the door even opened but because there's an old-fashioned latch on the other side he can use to lock the door with.

"That should buy us some time," he says, testing the handle.

Clarice digs her claws into his forearm. "Toby," she says, tugging at him like a child. "Toby, turn around."

Toby obeys. "Sweet Jesus."

Like the hall outside, teak panels form the walls, and mahogany boards form the floor. At the far end of the room are three full-length windows, all of which are covered by drawn curtains. A large, leather couch sits in the middle of the room and faces a hearth where a fire steadily burns. Tucked away at opposite corners are two heavy, closed doors. But none of that is what shocks the hell out of him. None of that is causing Toby's stomach to cramp. In front of the couch is a human-skin rug. A Matt, human-skin rug. His head is facing the fireplace, eyes glaring and mouth snarling, while his arms and legs are splayed to each side.

Clarice covers her mouth with her hand. "I think I'm going to be sick."

"Don't look." Toby hurries to the windows, and as he makes his way across the room, he tells himself that the bowl sitting on a table filled with human teeth, and the waste paper basket made from someone's foot, aren't real. By the time he gets to the other side of the room, he's done a fine job of buying into the delusion.

"God, I can't wait to see where we are," he says.

"You and me both."

Toby draws back the curtains, half expecting to see a close-up view of Saturn's rings or an alien, double sunset on the horizon. Instead what he's greeted with are countless skyscrapers, some not even a hundred feet away. Toby leans his head against the glass and goes up on his tiptoes. Down below, fifty, sixty stories maybe, people walk the streets. Cars attempt to navigate gridlock. Humanity bustles.

Clarice appears at his side. "Oh...my...god..." she says.

Toby bangs on the window with the flat of his palms. "Hey!"

Clarice punches him hard in the shoulder. "Are you out of your mind?" she whispers. Her eyes are wide, and her voice trembles. "They'll hear you!"

Toby curses and rubs his shoulder. For such a tight little package, Clarice packs mean punch. "Sorry," he replies with a sheepish grin. "Got a little excited."

Clarice shakes her head and mumbles under her breath. "It's not real, anyway. It's a fancy projection screen."

Toby leans close to the window. It takes a moment for his eyes to notice, but when they do, he can see the tiny pixels on the other side of the glass. "Must be to keep the up the ambiance."

"Yeah, but we need to go," she says. "Can't sit. Can't wait."

"I'll try this door. You get the other." Toby says and heads to his right. He presses his ear to the door and after ensuring that he can hear no sounds from the other side, he pushes the handle and the door swings open.

There's no light coming from inside, but the light from the den and fireplace is more than enough to tell Toby that this is a bedroom. He can easily see the oak canopy bed that fills half the room. He can even make out the matching nightstands and dressers inside. Thankfully, both the bed and room are unoccupied.

"Bedroom," Toby says.

"Can't tell," says Clarice, who is standing across the den and peering inside another dark room. "That," she says, tentatively stepping into the shadows, "might be a light switch."

Toby watches her disappear into the dark. There's a thump and a distinctively feminine cursing. A bright, white light then pours out and spills into the den.

Toby smiles. "Nice!"

Clarice, still unseen, screams.

Toby rushes in, fists up and ready to hammer whatever freak of the galaxy happens to be inside. What Toby is greeted with is anything but alien. Inside is a warm office with high beam ceilings and a solid oak desk with a high-back leather chair. Next to that chair is a man who's dressed in a pinstriped, charcoal, Gucci business suit. His hair is short, trimmed, and gelled. His shoes, black leather, are immaculately polished. In one hand he wields a fountain pen, and in the other, he holds a monogrammed portfolio. He has a serious look on his face, and if Toby wasn't absolutely certain the man was stuffed and dead, he'd swear the guy was about to close a multi-billion dollar deal.

Toby's attention snaps back to the here and now, and he turns to his secretary. "Clarice?"

Clarice stands rooted in place, slowly shaking her head. Mascara-filled tears stain her cheeks, and her hands weakly cover her mouth. "Nick..."

"Nick?" echoes Toby. He repeats the name in his mind a few more times, looking back and forth between Clarice and the stuffed man until the name finally registers. Toby puts an arm around her shoulders and leads her out. "I'm sorry."

They get no more than a few paces out of the room before she collapses into him, sobbing heavily.

Toby hugs her tight. There's nothing he can say or do. He knows that. He knows better than to even try.

"I always told myself he got away," she says, her face still buried into his chest. "He was supposed to get away. Every day I said it. Every minute, I told myself it would be okay."

Her hands claw his back, but Toby doesn't let her go. Not even when he feels his skin tear.

"How could I be so stupid?" she asks.

"We all tell ourselves things that aren't true," he says.

Clarice snorts. "I guess we do."

The two stand in silence for a few minutes, sharing the embrace, before Toby pulls back. "Clarice?" he says, tentatively. "Can I ask you something?"

Clarice sucks in a deep breath and clears her eyes. "About Nick?"

"Yeah."

"If you want."

"I thought you said he's the one that cut you."

"He did," she replies, looking away. "He did it to save me. He did it to keep them from shooting me—so I could escape."

Toby's brow furrows as he's not able to connect the dots. "How was that going to help?"

Clarice sniffs and shrugs. "Never had a specific plan," she replies. "It was only to buy time. No one wants to bag an ugly girl; we're not as prestigious, not worth as much."

"But that's what you were going to do to me," says Toby, still not following her logic, still hoping her deceased boyfriend knew of a way out. "You had to have had some sort of idea."

Clarice chokes on a snot-filled laugh. "It was a pretty crappy idea, to be honest. It was the only thing I could think to do that might keep you alive longer."

"There's got to be something he said, Clarice. Some way out."

"No," she says, shaking her head. A tidal wave of grief hits her full force, and she breaks down again. "I'm sorry, Toby. I'm so sorry. I've been here so long. Most of the time it's hard to think straight. I can't even count the seasons anymore."

Toby lifts her chin and locks eyes with her. "Try, Clarice. What did he say to you? What was the last thing he said?"

Clarice stares through him, and it's clear her mind is no longer in the room with him. "Oh, god," she says. Her body shudders uncontrollably, and her fingers clench his back. She sucks in her breath and bites down on her lip.

"What do you see, Clarice?"

"They're taking him," she says, eyes wide. "They're taking him, and he's still alive. They won't let go."

"He had to have said something. Think, Clarice."

Clarice shakes her head and buries her face into his shoulder. She takes a second to reply, but it's lost in a whimper.

"What did he say?"

Toby feels her swallow, feels her tighten her grip. "He said he loved me," she says.

Toby kisses the top of her head and squeezes her one last time. "We'll get out. I promise." The last part he tacks on for himself as much as for her.

"There you are," calls a voice from behind. "You must be so scared out in a big place like this."

Toby whips around to see Freddie standing in the doorway. In one hand, the alien is holding a small, cocked and loaded crossbow, and in the other, he's casually keeping a high-tech, multi-barrel rifle tucked under his armpit.

Toby straightens. Realizing there's nowhere to run, no point in trying either, he digs deep to stand his ground. "Going to kill us now?"

"Shhh, persie," Freddie says, slithering forward a few feet. His tentacle drifts over his shoulder and produces a Rice Krispies Treat. "Here you go, little fella. Don't be scared."

"Keep your goddamn treat to yourself," Toby replies.

Freddie extends the treat nonetheless. "This is all for your own good, Toby. Let's go home where it's safe."

Toby feels Clarice hide behind him. Her body stays close to his, and one of her arms wraps around his waist and holds him tight. Her distraction, however, is momentary. "Back where it's safe?" Toby says with a mocking laugh. "You shooting us is hardly safe."

Freddie shrugs. "It might not be me," he says. "Might be someone else. It's hard to say who bags who in this sport."

"This sport?" Toby repeats. "This isn't sporting in the least!"

"Oh, Toby," says Freddie with pity loud and clear in his voice. "If you were smart enough to understand the nature of things, you'd think differently. You're going to have to trust me on this."

"I don't trust anyone so heinous."

"Heinous?" Freddie says, clearly shocked and hurt at the allegation. "You seem a little smarter than the other persies, Toby, so I'll try and explain it to you. I provide a very noble service. I give you persies all that you want and more. I let you live out your dreams, and in return, I provide a safe, controlled environment for hunters to enjoy."

"If you really cared about giving us what we wanted, you'd let us go home."

"What? Back in the wild?" Freddie says. "Back where there's disease? Archaic medicine? How will you ever survive? I doubt you could even feed yourself anymore. No, no, Toby. Like I said, you're much better off here. I know what's best."

"Rot in hell."

"Now Toby," Freddie says, voice lowering. "I thought you could be civil about this. Besides, I don't need you to upset your mate, either."

Toby narrows his eyes. He wonders if he can clear the distance between the two before Freddie can get a shot off. "Stay away from her."

"Don't be like that," says Freddie. "I need her to deliver healthy babies so we can get our nursery restocked." He tosses the Rice Krispies Treat to the floor and uses his tentacle to whip out a little box. After giving it a few taps, a portal appears near the fireplace. "Come on," he says. "Enough of this. After all, the season is still going, and we can't have you running loose, can we?"

Toby doesn't budge. "The only place I'm going is home. My home. And I'm taking Clarice with me. So make it happen, or else..."

Freddie sighs and raises his rifle. "I don't want to have to shoot you here," he says. "It wouldn't be sporting, would it? And the maid will be in a tizzy if she has to clean up the mess."

A knife suddenly appears about a half inch from Toby's eye. Clarice, using her free hand, tightly grips his throat. "Leave him alone or I carve up his face," she says.

Toby stiffens. "Clarice? Can we talk about this?"

"Shut up," she says. Then, addressing Freddie, she says, "Now send us home."

Freddie, however, seems unconcerned at Clarice's behavior. In fact, if Toby would have to guess based on the alien's body language, he'd guess the alien was happy, ecstatic even. "Clarice! You *are* pregnant!" he says. "It's about time!"

In a flash, Freddie raises his handheld crossbow and fires. The bolt zips between Toby's legs, and he hears Clarice grunt. She loses her grip on his back and wobbles before falling to the floor.

Toby yells and charges forward, but Freddie spins to the side, allowing him to slip harmlessly past. Toby manages to stop himself before he crashes into the wall, but it's not the most grace-filled stop, and he stumbles as he spins around. To his surprise, Freddie's gun is no longer pointed at him. It's not even raised.

"Toby, Toby, Toby," Freddie says, shaking his head. "Why get so worked up? She's ugly."

Toby snarls and charges again. Like the first time, Freddie slips away, deftly avoiding the attack. This time, however, the alien counters with a grab and throw of his own. Before Toby realizes it, he's sent flying through the portal.

CHAPTER TWELVE

Toby rolls across Preser Tech's lobby floor and comes up in a low crouch. The portal through which he came is twenty feet away, and Toby has the urge to charge back through it. He has that urge, that is, right until Freddie comes through with his rifle shouldered and ready.

Toby dives for the nearest bit of cover, which happens to be the reception desk. An explosion rocks the ground where he was moments ago, shattering the tile and sending marble shrapnel in all directions.

"Bravo, Toby!" Freddie says. "Bravo, indeed!"

Toby crouches lower, trying to keep his head as far away from the top of the desk as possible. He glances left and right, looking for a way out, looking for a way he can reach the elevators or stairs without getting blasted. But the lobby is sparsely decorated, and he doesn't think he'd be able to round the divider in time.

"I've got an offer for you, Toby," says Freddie. "It's an offer you can't refuse."

Toby shakes his head. A moment passes, and it dawns on him that Freddie is expecting a reply. "Does this offer include me and Clarice leaving?" asks Toby.

Freddie laughs. "Why would I go and do something like that?" he says once he's calmed down. "Besides, what could that dirty home offer that you don't have here?"

"My wife and kids, for starters," Toby answers, "and me living."

Freddie laughs again. "You call that living?" he says. "I bet you'll say no when I offer you a promotion and raise. I'll even toss in another secretary too. Are you going to honestly say your wife and offspring can compete with that?"

Toby curses under his breath. There's no talking his way out of this. His eyes scan for an escape, but he still doesn't see a way out from behind the desk. What he does see, however, is Boris's belt nearby, complete with gun and mace.

"Well, Toby? What do you think?" Freddie calls out.

Toby tries to gauge where the alien is standing by his voice, and he thinks he can stretch and snag the deceased guard's gear without being seen. And so he does. Like a snake striking at its prey, Toby lunges, grabs the end of the belt, and snaps back.

"I got you now," he whispers to himself, pulling the revolver from its holster. But the moment he gets a look at the weapon, his heart drops. It's all he can do to keep from crying in despair. The weapon is not a weapon at all, merely a high-quality replica. The mace, too, is nothing more than an inexpensive, plastic tube. Still, Toby wonders if he could use the pistol as a club.

A two inch hole blows out of the desk, and the gun disintegrates.

"Time's almost up on these negotiations, Toby," says Freddie.

Toby, now sprawled across the floor, picks himself up and presses into the desk once again. He has no doubt that the alien missed him on purpose. "What do you want?"

"I lost valuable hunting time tracking you down," Freddie coolly replies. "I want a chase. A good one. Since it should be only the two of us here now, we can keep things interesting, yes? A true sportsman's challenge!"

"You want me to run?"

"I do," Freddie answers. "But make it a good one."

Toby smirks at the futility of it all. "How does this keep me alive long enough for that promotion, again?"

"The season is almost over, Toby," Freddie says. "Not even four hours left. Give me a good chase and survive long enough, and voila! You'll have your promotion, and I'll have the anticipation of tracking you down next season, a mighty stag with an even longer name tag than before! And if you survive that one, I'll promote you again. Just think, you might even make CEO one day."

"Do I get a head start?"

"I think it's only fair, don't you?" Freddie answers. "How about to the count of ten?"

Toby leaps to his feet and runs. He rockets around the divider and past the vending machines before Freddie reaches three. By the time the alien reaches ten, or so Toby guesses, he's up two flights of stairs with plenty of energy and wind to spare.

He exits the stairwell on the fourth floor, only because it's the only floor he feels he knows to any degree. He halts for a second and gawks at his surroundings. Several of the vending machines and water coolers are spattered with blood. A few are even still impaled by spears of varying lengths and thicknesses, and the carpet is stained in a dozen places. Contrasting this grisly scene, a sweet perfume hangs in the air, and the sounds of intense, primal sex drift down the hall. No doubt a porno is playing somewhere, another baited trap.

Toby grabs one of the spears and tries to pull it free from the wall, but it doesn't budge. Neither does the next or the next. Cursing, Toby runs to the break room he saw when he first arrived, hoping to scavenge some sort of weapon there.

He ducks into the room a few seconds later. It's small, with a single round table in one corner and a couple of plastic chairs nearby. But it has cabinets, lots of cabinets. Unfortunately, as Toby throws open their doors and rips through their contents, all he can find are paper plates, cups, and napkins. The last cabinet mocks his struggle, for inside there are boxes of plastic sporks, and not even the sturdy kind.

"Oh Toby!" Freddie calls, his voice coming from down the hall. "Don't make this too easy!"

Toby glances out of the room, but doesn't see his alien pursuer. Freddie must have gotten off the elevators and is purposely toying with him. Whatever the alien's motives are, Toby has no intention of sticking around and runs down the hall in the opposite direction. Though he tries to move lightly on his feet, his footsteps sound so loudly in his ears he figures he might as well be a rampaging elephant. Too bad he isn't, Toby thinks. He could use a big pair of tusks and a killer stampede right about now.

Toby ducks into the cubicle farm, slipping through the doors as quietly as he can. Like the outer hall, the farm shows signs of a massive hunt. Cubicles are spattered with blood, and the rug is beyond any steam cleaner's ability to repair. The radio hisses white noise, and to Toby's left, a coffee pot lies on its side.

"Hot damn," he says, picking it up. His enthusiasm fades, however, when he sees the pot isn't made of glass, but plastic, and there's no way he'll be able to get a decent, stabbing shard out of it.

"If there's one thing I hate, Toby, it's predictable game."

Toby spins around at the sound of Freddie's voice. Though the alien is near, Toby sees that the doors are still closed. Not wanting to be there when they open, Toby moves through the farm, hunched over, as quickly as he can. He glances in each workspace he passes, hoping to see something he can use, but comes up empty each and every time.

Toby hears the double doors open and close, and he can practically feel Freddie's presence in the air.

"Toby," Freddie calls. "I'm afraid at this rate you're not looking like promotion material."

Toby stops when he spies the handful of empty pens he sucked dry earlier. He hadn't given them much thought when he was trying to ward off being drugged, but now that he's looking at them again, he notices that in the middle of four, cheap Bics is the broken shell of a well-made fountain pen.

Toby grabs the pen and lightly jabs it into his chest. It's not the best weapon in the world, but it's sharp and sturdy. Toby thinks he could get at least one good stab with it. Maybe even three or four if he went for Freddie's eyes.

"I'm getting bored, Toby," Freddie says.

Toby, still hiding in the farm, screams and grabs his left shoulder after the crisp staccato note of a rifle shot. Blood pours down his arm, and he doubles over in pain. He runs blindly with his left hand nearly dragging on the floor. He's panicked, and he knows it. But he can't think straight, and he doesn't dare stop moving. He has to get out of the farm, and he has to do it now.

Toby bursts through the farm's exit doors and stumbles into the wall. He pushes off, leaving a bright red hand print where he hit, and runs back to the stairwell. A second before he starts his ascent, he decides to try the elevator. Running up the stairs will cost him strength and provide an exact trail to follow.

If the elevator is there, he figures, it might buy him some time while Freddie figures out which floor he got off on.

To Toby's relief, the elevator is waiting on the fourth floor, and the instant he hits the button, the doors slide open with a friendly ding. Toby half falls, half staggers inside and hammers the button to the top, the twelfth floor.

The elevator rises, and Toby wipes his forehead, trading the sweat on his brow for the large amounts of blood on his hand. He catches sight of himself in the reflection of the brass plate that houses the buttons and stares. Though the wound to his shoulder is not life threatening, it's still made him a bloody mess. He's such a mess, in fact, that if he didn't know better, he'd have thought he'd already been killed.

The elevator dings, and the doors open. Toby spills out on the twelfth floor, his heart racing and his breath labored. The elevator doors close behind him, and the floor indicator above shows the elevator on a rapid descent down, a descent that stops at the fourth floor.

"Get moving, Toby," he says, staring in disbelief as the elevator begins its ascent. Five. Six. Seven and climbing. "I said, get moving!"

Toby finally obeys himself and rockets down the hall. Most of the doors along the way are closed, but a few are open, revealing private offices. Toby smears his hand on each one, hoping it will cause Freddie to check them all and buy him much needed time.

The hall bends, and Toby wonders if the layout is similar to the fourth floor. But after the second bend, he sees that it's not. The hall comes to an abrupt halt at a set of double doors. Above those doors is a plaque that reads: BOARD ROOM.

A thump, muffled, but distinct, comes from inside. Toby wipes his palms on his pants, quietly cracks open the doors, and peers inside. A large, polished conference table sits in the middle of the room, while a dozen leather chairs are spaced haphazardly around. On the far wall is a mural of a city skyline, complete with white, puffy clouds and a bright yellow sun. About half way into the room, off to the side, is a portal. Toby would have run for it immediately, if it hadn't been for the twelve dead office execs laying on the floor, all in a nice, neat row and the two Freddie and three Mr. Squid look-a-likes that were busy hauling other kills out of the office.

Toby quietly backs off the board room doors and peers around the corner, back the way he came. He sees Freddie step out from one of the side offices. Thankfully, Toby ducks back before the aliens sees him.

He's trapped. Toby knows this. He looks down at the broken fountain pen gripped tightly in his hands. "You're not going to get me without a fight," he mumbles to himself. Toby looks up, looks to the boardroom and back down to his meager weapon before adding softly, "But there are alternatives to fighting."

CHAPTER THIRTEEN

Freddie tracks Toby's blood trail to the board room with ease. He reaches the doors and shifts his grip on his rifle. It's time for a quick, clean kill, he decides. He is a little disappointed with Toby, as he did hope for a better hunt. The persie could have at least tried to double back once or twice, but alas, not every hunt can be perfect.

Freddie slithers into the board room and immediately spies his prey, but he doesn't shoot. Instead, he lowers his weapon and resigns himself to the fact that the chase is over. Toby's lifeless body lies face down alongside eight other kills, his back covered in blood and proud hunters standing near.

"Enjoy the day?" Freddie asks as his patrons turn to greet him.

"As always," one of them replies.

Freddie nods. "Be sure to check those with the warden."

"Of course," says another.

"Don't forget, we have an excellent taxidermist and butcher for all your gaming needs," he adds.

"Porxil is the finest," says a third.

Freddie smiles and gives an impromptu, two-fingered human salute, his customary goodbye to all his patrons, and heads through the portal. He passes through the freezer section without as much as a glance here or there, and decides to stop at the bar to enjoy a bottle of wine and some good company before heading to his room. Maybe he can buy Toby when they're done with him. After all, he got a good price on Matt.

As Freddie returns to his suite, he hums a few bars of <u>Madame Butterfly</u> and locks the door behind him. The fire burns low, barely more than hot coals on a bed of ash. But the light they give is enough to pierce the darkness and show Clarice still crumpled on the floor.

Freddie smiles. The tranq he hit her with should keep her down at least till the next morning. There's plenty of time, he knows, to relax another hour or two, perhaps order some room service before going back to work and wrapping up another successful season.

The last thought, however, troubles Freddie. While it's true that the preserve enjoyed one of its busiest hunts as of late, and both his customers and his stock holders are deliriously happy, two annoyances prick at his mind and keep him from enjoying a perfect evening.

First, Clarice had gotten ahold of an actual knife, which meant his staff had been slacking when it came to promoting a safe environment. After all, the last thing he needs is a patron getting hurt. His insurance company would love to raise his rates.

The second thing that digs under Freddie's skin is the fact that he wasn't the one to bag Toby, even though he had every opportunity to do so. Freddie scolds himself for toying with his game, but he's also quick to remind himself that at the very least, his customers are happy. No doubt, he adds, one customer is very happy, having bagged the VP of Communications and Investment Opportunities for the Acquisition of Hostile Companies. With that in mind, Freddie slithers to the window and looks outside.

Below him the city bustles with activity, despite the late night. Lights fill buildings as far as his eyes can see, and countless whites and reds mark a sea of automobile traffic on the streets. "Plenty more," Freddie says to himself, tapping the glass. "Plenty bigger."

Freddie reaches over and flips a switch on the wall. It takes his eyes a half second to adjust to the bright lights, and half that to spy the man standing in the bedroom doorway.

"Toby!" Freddie exclaims. "You've survived the season! A promotion is in order!"

"As far as I can tell, the season's still going," says Toby in a low tone, clutching a broken fountain pen. "And where I come from, you don't promote game animals."

Freddie twitches his fangs. "I see," he says. "Then one of us will be a kill to tell the grandkids about. The other will sleep well tonight—very well indeed. Now, Toby, en garde!"

EPILOGUE

A timely yawn stops the story. "Did you sleep well, Grampy?" asks the smallest of three grandchildren.

"I did," he replies. The fire burns low in the hearth and casts long shadows in the den. "I slept very well that night."

Another yawn hangs in the air and is followed by the rustling of sleeping bags. "When did you get your robot arm?" asks the middle child.

Before he can answer, the oldest adds, "And what happened to Clarice?"

Sitting in a rocker, Toby stares at the antique, broken fountain pen in his hand for a moment before taking to his feet. He winces once from old age and old wounds before kissing and tucking his grandchildren into their bedrolls. "All of that," he says, "is a story for another night."

ACKNOWLEDGEMENTS

To all the aliens who generously donated their time so I could understand how Preser Tech operates...

To my slew of readers who went over countless drafts and helped shape Office Preserves into a fun romp...

To my editor, Crystal Watanabe, who helped see it through its final leg of work...

And most of all, to my wife, Mary Beth, who keeps reading my stuff at my request and somehow hasn't been driven away.

ABOUT THE AUTHOR

When not writing, Galen Surlak-Ramsey has been known to throw himself out of an airplane, teach others how to throw themselves out of an airplane, take pictures of the deep space, and wrangle his four children somewhere in Southwest Florida.

He also manages to pay the bills as a chaplain for a local hospice.

Drop by his website www.galensurlak.com to see what other books he has out, what's coming out, and check out the newsletter (well, sign up for the newsletter and get access to awesome goodies, contests, exclusive content, etc.).

ABOUT THE PUBLISHER

Tiny Fox Press LLC
5020 Kingsley Road
North Port, FL 34287

www.tinyfoxpress.com